"Why Don't You Take A Few Chances?"

Jesse leaned closer to Angela.

"I do take chances!" she retorted. "Walking onstage in front of the kind of audience that comes to see you and singing folk music is taking chances enough to qualify anyone as a fool!"

Jesse silently watched the play of emotions on her face: resentment, anger, defensiveness, mixed with something vulnerable enough to prick his conscience. There was a hint of unleashed passion that drew him like a desert wanderer to a watering hole and wouldn't let him back off.

"You hired me to play it safe!" she burst out when he didn't answer. Her voice rose defensively. "Why are you pushing me?" Her eyes were dark with emotion she'd kept rigidly controlled.

"Maybe I just want to see what you'd do if you stopped holding yourself back, Angel—if you just once let your emotions take control."

Dear Reader:

I hope you've been enjoying 1989, our "Year of the Man" at Silhouette Desire. Every one of the twelve authors who are contributing a *Man of the Month* has created a very special someone for your reading pleasure. Each man is unique, and each author's style and characterization give you a different insight into her man's story.

From January to December, 1989 will be a twelve-month extravaganza spotlighting one book each month with special cover treatment as a tribute to the Silhouette Desire hero—our *Man of the Month*!

Created by your favorite authors, these men are utterly irresistible. Love, betrayal, greed and revenge are all part of Lucy Gordon's dramatic *Vengeance Is Mine*, featuring Luke Harmon as Mr. May, and I think you'll find Annette Broadrick's Quinn McNamara . . . *Irresistible*! Coming in June.

Don't let these men get away!

Yours,

Isabel Swift
Senior Editor & Editorial Coordinator

25

FRANCES
WEST

HONKY TONK ANGEL

SILHOUETTE *Desire*

Published by Silhouette Books New York

America's Publisher of Contemporary Romance

SILHOUETTE BOOKS
300 East 42nd St., New York, N.Y. 10017

ISBN: 0-373-05496-3

First Silhouette Books printing May 1989

FRANCES WEST

has been making up stories for as long as she can remember. When she's not thinking about what she's just read, what she's writing or what she might like to write, she's traveling, studying ballet or playing her mandolin. Frances and her family live in Massachusetts.

HOPE AND DREAMS

All I am is hope and dreams
Tryin' to live on lies and schemes.
Love is never what it seems.
I never get it right.

I know that what we had was real,
I know the way it made me feel,
But even love can never steal
The darkness from the night.

Hope and dreams and hangin' on,
Waiting for the light of dawn,
Knowing what you had is gone
And never knowing why.

You only do the best you can,
You never get to see the plan.
The thing I've come to understand
Is how to say goodbye.

SERITA'S SONG

She taught me how to play what she was singing,
On a summer day beneath a big blue sky.
I was greener than the springtime in the valley,
But I wanted her to teach me how to fly.

The road beyond that dusty blue horizon
Gave me longings that I couldn't seem to lose,
And everything I ever knew of freedom,
Was the cloud of dust that lifted from her shoes.

One

Angela Trent glanced out at the near-empty auditorium, drew a deep breath—and caught a distracting movement at the side of the stage, in the wings that should have been empty. Her glance flicked toward it.

At the edge of the curtain, a tall, lean figure took a step toward her. He set down his battered guitar case, straightened, and pushed his black cowboy hat back on his head.

He was here.

The realization struck her with the blunt force of unexpected stage fright. Angela's palms were suddenly damp on the neck of her guitar, and her throat was as tight as the steel strings of a bluegrass mandolin.

The man who stood watching her was a consummate musician. Talented, accomplished, charismatic...and more than that. He was Jesse Adam Wilson, the Texas Drifter, and he was legendary.

"Don't let me hold things up." The rough, low-pitched, Texas-accented voice held the timbre of sensuality that had been selling record albums for fifteen years.

Angela's gaze was drawn with magnetic fascination. The cool interest on his face wasn't softened by any hint of a smile. The hands that could hold a guitar with the arrogant assurance of fame were pushed into the pockets of his worn jeans. The long body that, on stage, seemed charged with enough energy to fire up an entire audience, now slouched against the proscenium arch. He crossed one boot in front of the other and waited.

From the auditorium, Jesse's manager, Jack O'Malley, commented, "Glad you could make it, Jesse. We were just about to begin."

Angela forced herself to look away, out at the dark concert hall. It was unoccupied except for the man in the front row who had just spoken and who had set up this audition. Her performance would decide if she'd be opening for Jesse Adam Wilson on his next tour. She wiped one palm against her hip.

Once, three years ago, Serita must have stood here in just this way, to audition for Jesse Adam Wilson.

Serita had gotten the job.

She took another breath, strummed a chord on her six-string Martin, and willed herself to sing. The mellow notes of the guitar led into the music. Her voice, trained by years of professional demands, responded to her will.

The melody was simple, familiar. She'd chosen it for its universal popularity and because it was well suited to her range, she let her voice flow, over the words, in a clear soprano that carried the tune through to the end, as it had many times before, with perfect control and pitch.

When the final note had dissolved in the near-empty auditorium, Angela straightened her shoulders, then glanced, again, toward the man standing in the wings.

He pushed himself away from the stage support and ambled toward her. "You have a voice like an angel, Angel," he said softly.

The breath she'd been holding escaped her lungs with a swift release of tension. She started to smile.

Jesse Wilson's dark eyes, as black as the thick, straight hair that brushed the collar of his faded shirt, narrowed. His mouth widened in the cynical, friend-of-the-devil smile that was known to country-and-western fans from Juneau, Alaska to Macon Corners, Georgia.

"But you sing like a Girl Scout," he added.

Angela's tentative smile died a quick, painful death. She stared at him. Jesse Wilson returned the stare. Taking his time, he let that gaze drift down from her wide, gray-green eyes, straight nose with a sprinkling of freckles across its bridge, expressive, curving mouth, to her ash blond hair, loose on her shoulders, her oversize white blouse and not-at-all-oversize jeans. His attention lingered for a moment on the curve of her backside before he looked back at her face.

Angela Trent swallowed, met his eyes, and raised her chin. "I sing like this music is supposed to be sung."

"Do y'now? And what makes you think you know how it's supposed to be sung?"

"Because I've heard it all my life. And because—because I feel it."

His look was level and challenging. "Okay, then, Angel, sing me another one."

She nodded once, nervously, toward Jesse Adam Wilson then strummed a chord. She made an adjustment to a string, went into the introduction to a song she'd written herself.

The music, as always, caught her up and took her with it, unerringly, to the place where she'd learned to sing, the green, rolling East Nebraska farm country where she'd been born and grown up, where her grandmother had patted out pie dough and accompanied the work with a song. She had known all her neighbors, and been free from the time she was seven to walk as far as she liked along the quiet roads bordered by rolling prairie, dotted with tiny, exquisite wild-flowers and forested ridges laced with small streams.

When the last notes of "My Home is in this Heartland" had drifted over the hall, there was a moment of charged silence. Its tension burned like fox fire in the dark auditorium, before the silence was broken by a flat comment from the front row. "She's good, Jesse."

Jesse Wilson glanced toward the speaker. Then, as if he were considering something, he turned his head to study the guitar he'd left in the wings.

The case was battered and road worn, its edges frayed from use. Hanging from the handle was an Indian necklace of eagle feathers. Angela recognized it. It belonged to Serita Black, her cousin, who had toured with Jesse for three years.

Had belonged to her. Serita was dead.

And Jesse needed a new act to open for him on his upcoming tour.

He looked back at her and let out a long breath of cynical acceptance. "You may be a Girl Scout, Angel, but you can sing."

He turned and walked off the stage, stopped to pick up his guitar case, and disappeared behind the curtain.

Angela watched disbelievingly, her hands still on her own guitar, her fingers already forming the opening chord of her next song. She looked toward the auditorium, confused, wondering if she should begin the tune, then glanced again at the dark wings.

"Well, that's it." Jack O'Malley's voice was wry.

She turned a blank look in his direction.

"When do you want to meet the band?" he asked.

Serita Black was still part of this band.
And Angela Trent was still on audition.

The truth of the observation hung uneasily over her introductions to the band members. Even in the bright, contemporary suite of a downtown Dallas hotel, where Jack O'Malley had organized an informal party, she felt out of place—like the photographer at a wedding. Invited, but not part of the family.

You've been invited to audition, she'd been told by the small Nebraska studio where she'd cut her two albums. The message had been uttered with surprise. Word had been out, in the industry, that the Jesse Adam Wilson Band was looking for an opening act. They were willing to consider a single performer, but when she'd told her studio she wanted to try for the job, there had been some skeptical looks. A Nebraska folksinger and a country-and-western star like Jesse Wilson would be an unlikely partnership. She hadn't expected to be hired, but she'd had to try. For reasons she hadn't fully analyzed, she'd had to stand on that stage and sing for Jesse Adam Wilson—Serita's sponsor. And, everyone knew, Serita's lover.

She glanced across the half-crowded room toward the man who had been her cousin's lover, conscious of her own physical reaction to him. He was leaning against the bathroom door, cowboy hat pushed low on his forehead, black shirt with silver snaps tucked into ancient jeans. He had a bottle of whiskey in one hand, held carelessly by the neck. At his feet was the ubiquitous guitar case, adorned with Serita's eagle-feather necklace.

He caught Angela's look and their eyes locked for a moment. Then his mouth curved in the outlaw's smile she'd seen on countless record albums and he raised the bottle in a silent, half-mocking toast. The gesture was unsettling. The uneasy knot in her chest tightened.

From the other side of the room, Jack O'Malley looked up, crossed the thick carpet toward her and held out a can of light beer. He smiled neutrally. "Have you met everyone?"

"Yes, I think so." Angela took the beer with murmured thanks and turned her attention to the ten or twelve band members in the room, trying to fit the names to all the faces.

Carlos Riverra, the big, laconic, dark-haired drummer, leaned against a corner of the table laden with barbecued ribs and burritos. Despite his obvious Mexican background, he'd opted for the Texas ribs. Beside him, a good size pile of bones was heaped on a paper plate surrounded by empty beer cans. Frank West, the fiddle player, was crouched in front of the entertainment system, examining the jacket of the Willie Nelson CD that was playing at almost full volume. He bounced on the heels of his sneakers in time to the music, curly hair moving with his actions, his thin body as attuned to rhythm as it was to breathing.

Her glance moved again to Jesse. He tipped up the bottle, drank from it, then nodded at them. Jack O'Malley made no comment, but Angela could sense the manager's disapproval in the set of his burly shoulders and the thinning of his lips. She shot him a quick, puzzled glance. He returned the look with one of his own. His expression was steady but it held no information, and no clue as to how to handle the odd tension that reverberated in the room like an unresolved chord at the end of a song.

Angela took a tentative sip from her can. Serita would have dominated this informal gathering the way she'd dominated a stage. With her black hair, scarlet lipstick, the striking high cheekbones of her Sioux ancestry emphasized by beads, feathers and buckskin, she would have defied this vague unease with the recklessness that was Serita's trademark. When put on stage, as it had been, that recklessness was a vibrant legacy. Beside it, Angela Trent felt like a pale watercolor, painted in washed tones of gray.

She felt Jack's silently assessing gaze taking in her reactions. *This was still part of the audition.* The thought added its own coil of nervousness.

A rangy, thirty-year-old cowboy that she remembered as the bass player aimed a boyish grin in her direction and stepped toward her. "Ol' Mother Hen O'Malley been givin' you a hard time, honey?" he asked.

She smiled back at the openly admiring grin and the blue eyes. "No, he's been giving me a beer."

"Huh. Y'call that a beer?"

She glanced down at her can of light beer, then looked up again with a shrug and a smile. "Yes. What would you call it?"

The bass player raised an eyebrow at Jack. "I'd call it our manager's idea of a subtle suggestion." He turned his high-powered grin toward Angela. "We drink too much. And we party too much. And it's givin' us a *b-a-a-a-d* reputation."

Jack smiled back a little acidly. "And it's losing you some concert bookings. Don't leave that off the list." He nodded to Angela, gave the bass player a level stare, and said, "Excuse me. I've got to see if we need more food."

"Git some more ribs, will ya?" The boyish grin seemed unchastened, but the shrug was philosophical as the bass player turned back to Angela. "Jack's a good manager. Knows what he's talkin' about. We don't need to lose any more bookings."

She paused, surprised, assimilating the information. "How many have you lost?"

"Five in the past two weeks."

"Five?"

"Yeah. And some of us need the revenue, ya know?" He shrugged again. "Leavin' Jesse out of it. He don't care."

Angela glanced toward Jesse and frowned.

The bass player followed her gaze, then drank again, tilting the can up to drain it. He grinned at her. "But you're gonna change all that, aren't ya, honey? Give us a squeaky clean reputation, keep the fans from bustin' up the concert halls...."

Angela's hand halted in the act of raising her beer to her lips, and the tension she felt in this room suddenly focused into something real enough to feel in the pit of her stomach. Her eyes flicked to Jack O'Malley, standing by the food table looking over the offerings, to Jesse, leaning in the doorway, the bottle dangling from his fingers, back to the man in front of her. "*I'm* going to change all that?" she asked carefully.

"Yeah." He nodded. "That's what Jack thinks. We need a good influence. Someone more...ah...civilized than Rita. So the crowds won't get so rowdy. You know, so we can keep things cooled out before Jesse comes on and gets 'em worked up." He took a swallow from his can. "Crowd control. That's you, honey."

"That's—" She broke off.

There was a long moment of silence.

"Angela," she said, finally.

"What?"

"The name is Angela."

"Oh. Okay, An-ge-la." He mouthed the syllables as if he were a good-natured uncle teaching a child how to pronounce a difficult word.

She took a breath and glanced down at her hands. "I...don't remember your name."

"Hank Martin. You can call me Hank." He grinned again, assessing and appreciative. "Or you can call me honey, if you want."

An automatic smile tilted her lips, but her eyes kept their look of wary concentration. "What have your fans been doing?"

"Aw, nothin' too unusual. It's just that...Jesse's been wild since Rita died. Like I said, he doesn't care. He wouldn't even care if we didn't get work. It was just Rita's benefit concert gettin' canceled that made him decide to notice. Otherwise, he don't give a damn." He shook his head, smiling. "He just cuts loose on stage. And the crowds tend to get a little . . . rowdy, y'know?"

"Like—what?"

"Aww, yellin', dancin', booze." He studied her a moment, his mouth quirked. "Not used to rough crowds, huh?"

She wondered what he expected her to say. Her gaze flicked involuntarily toward Jesse again and she realized he was still watching her. His cowboy hat was tipped up just enough so that he could see across the room. The anxiety in her midsection jelled into a flicker of resistance. "No, I'm not used to rough crowds."

"Didn't think so." Hank Martin shook his empty beer can, then upended it to get the last drop. "Well, welcome to the big bad world, honey." He gave her an undimmed smile. "You want another beer?"

"No, thanks," she said.

She didn't even want the one she had. She set the can down on a windowsill and turned back to the party, to catch a sidelong look in her direction from Jack O'Malley. She had the feeling they were all going to discuss her after she'd left.

There was a small balcony off one side of the room. She headed for it, let herself out through the French doors and stood in the dark at the edge of the railing. Looking out over the lights of downtown Dallas, she fought something that felt inappropriately like stage fright. The tension in her stomach churned into anger.

She told herself the feeling was irrational. What did she have to be angry about? That she didn't like the reasons they'd hired her? That they were going to discuss her? Well, why shouldn't they? That's what auditions are for.

She'd been through her share of them.

But never on the level of this one. The anger she felt now, she knew, was fed by the anxiety of comparison. She was out of her league. She wasn't used to the kind of crowds attracted by Jesse Wilson: their size, their behavior or the burden of recognition they put on their idols. She wasn't used to fame or notoriety or the life that went with them. Serita's life.

She leaned her elbows on the railing, staring out at the city lights.

Serita's life.

Serita's life was why she was here, wasn't it?

Because Serita had been her cousin. Because Angela had loved her, and yet had known almost nothing about her adult life except what was printed in the papers and the rock magazines.

She should have known.

There was a sound behind her as the door opened, then slid closed. A tall, back-lit figure stepped out onto the balcony.

"You don't like the present company? Or you just can't resist the lights of Dallas from the eighteenth floor?"

The Texas drawl was Jesse's.

He took two steps to the railing, then leaned one hip on it, the bottle of whiskey still clutched in his hand, held loosely by the neck, as if he'd forgotten he still had it. He had an easy, graceful way of moving that emphasized the hard body and the harsh lines of the face.

His mouth curved up at both corners in a smile that had been famous when Angela was still in Junior High, and she felt a tingle of physical response shimmer up her spine. It wasn't difficult to see what had so attracted Serita. She could feel it herself: elemental, instinctive and visceral. Close up, his sexuality was even more potent than on stage.

She acknowledged her own reaction but set it aside, and made herself meet his eyes. She had to tip her head up to do it.

"I've never seen Dallas from the eighteenth floor. Or from any floor. I've never been here."

"No? Where have you been?"

"Nebraska. Iowa. California. I did a tour in New England last year."

He tipped his hat farther back on his head.

"In coffee houses, mostly," she persisted. "And church basements. A few small concert halls." She glanced out over the lighted city, then looked back at Jesse, her gaze direct and unequivocal. "I've made two albums. The second one did a little better than break even. I've never played to more than five hundred people at one time."

He shrugged. "You get used to it."

"There are a lot of singers who are already used to it."

"So?"

"So I guess I'd like to know why you picked me."

He swirled the bottle around, but didn't drink from it. Amber liquid reflected the muted light from the doors. "You didn't get the job because you're Rita's cousin, if that's what you're asking."

"Why did I get it, then?"

"I told you that yesterday." He settled more lazily against the railing, leaning casually over eighteen floors of the hotel. "You can sing. You've been around enough to know what you're doing." His gaze swept down to her feet, then, taking its time, back up again. "You're not hard to look at." The familiar desperado's grin crept into his face. "Matter of fact, Angel, you're downright easy to look at."

She felt again the flutter that was half nervousness and half attraction—and stiffened against it. "I'm a singer. What I look like has nothing to do with it."

Jesse Wilson let out a snort of skepticism. "Don't kid yourself, Angel. What you look like has everything to do with it. People want to hear a pretty voice, they can listen to the choir on Sunday morning. When they come to a concert, they want more than that. They want the voice, the looks—and they want someone to pick 'em up by the gut and make 'em feel something. Something they wouldn't likely be thinkin' about in church." His eyes drifted down to her backside again, the suggestion blatant, half-insolent, pushing for a reaction in a way that she recognized as some sort of challenge.

In spite of herself, Angela felt heat creep into her face. She ignored it, turned toward him, and leaned her hip on the railing in deliberate imitation of his posture. "I hear that the people who come to your concerts haven't been *acting* like churchgoers, either."

His eyes assessed her face for a second. "Hank likes to talk."

"It wouldn't have taken me long to find out that you've been having concerts canceled. Or that Jack O'Malley decided what this tour needed was someone to keep the fans under control."

"Nope, I suppose it wouldn't."

She took a deep breath, her eyes fixed on Jesse's face, her lips pursed to say words she hadn't quite formulated.

"What's the matter?" he asked her. "Scared you can't handle the job?"

She turned back toward the railing, leaned her elbows on it, and admitted, honestly, "Yes."

Jesse moved a few inches closer to her. "Shoot straight from the hip, do you, Angel?"

"That's the way we do it in church basements."

He let out a huff of breath that wasn't quite a chuckle. "I think you might have something that'll take you farther than the local church basement," he said softly, the words a low growl of approval. "Of course, you won't know that unless you give it a try."

"I never said I wasn't going to give it a try."

"Glad to hear it, Angel." The outlaw's mocking grin appeared again, and the dark eyes played over her face, lingering on the wide mouth. "Any time you want to practice gettin' out of church, you let me know."

There was a terse silence. "*Angela*," she said. "Angela Trent."

"Angela. Meaning you're no honky-tonk angel?"

"No, I'm not."

He gave a rasp of cynical, whiskey-rough laughter. "Too bad."

"I thought you hired me to clean up the band's reputation."

"That's why *Jack* hired you." He adjusted his hat, but he didn't spell out the implication of his statement.

The silver snap at the open collar of his shirt strained against the material as he shifted his elbow on the railing, one broad shoulder hunched to take his weight. The shirt looked to be tailored for him. It narrowed to the line of his hips with casual ease that emphasized the well muscled torso, the narrow waist. Angela brushed her hair back from her shoulder in unconscious response, then, slowly, put her arm to the railing.

Without warning, Jesse reached up to run the back of his hand along the curve of her cheek. Her eyes widened, and she tipped her head away.

"Just wanted to see if it was as soft as it looks." The suggestive smile flickered. "It is," he said.

Her expression was wary. "I'm not Serita, Jesse."

Jesse let out a long breath that seemed to exhale the Texas flippancy and replace it with something harder and less easy to read. A muscle in his jaw clenched while he studied her, leaning on the railing in the darkness. "I don't think I'm in danger of gettin' you mixed up with Serita."

His eyes were so dark they looked black. His mouth was savage and sensual and, somehow, as mesmerizing as any she'd ever seen. Her breath caught in her throat, and she was aware, suddenly, of a thread of fear in her chest. There *was* danger here. But Jesse getting her mixed up with Serita didn't define it. Not by a long shot.

She curled her fingers into the concrete railing, as the sudden, vivid image of Jesse and Serita, together, flashed into her mind. "I guess you knew her better than anyone else," she said, her voice unnaturally taut.

He was silent a moment. He didn't bother with a direct answer. "She lived with your family for a couple of years, didn't she?"

"Yes. After her mother died."

Jesse nodded. "You must have been—what? Eight? Nine?"

"Eight."

There was a silence. Jesse didn't move.

"She didn't get along with my parents," Angela said finally. "She was always in trouble. Always getting caught. It seemed like she didn't care if she got caught." The ghost of a smile flickered over her mouth. "I was just a kid. I couldn't understand why anyone wouldn't care about getting caught."

The material of Jesse's shirt rasped against the railing as he shifted.

"We didn't have much use for each other," she went on. "She thought I was just a pain-in-the-neck little brat." She ran her fingers along the concrete edge of the railing, taking in a breath. "But she taught me how to play the guitar. I badgered her into it. We fought like cats and dogs, over everything, every possible point of contention. But when she played and sang..." Angela's quick, expressive sigh ruffled the silence, then vanished into it as tracelessly as wind over a prairie landscape fallow with the past season's plantings.

"Yeah," Jesse said into the silence. The word held undercurrents of meaning he didn't need to spell out.

She sensed his movement as he leaned his back against the railing, and turned her head toward him. "Hank said her benefit concert was canceled."

"Yeah."

"The benefit for Indian Education, that you do in South Dakota?"

Jesse stared down at the bottle again, but didn't raise it to his mouth. The bottle was a prop, she thought with sudden insight. Like his black hat and his lawless Texas image.

"This would have been the fifth year you'd done the concert, wouldn't it?" she asked.

He slanted her a look that held bitterness, hard determination, and something that could have been a shadow of pain. "This *will* be the fifth year we do it." The voice wasn't loud, but there was an intensity she couldn't miss. "We left two weeks free on the tour to reschedule it, when we'll be up near South Dakota. That's Jack's job—to get it booked." The determination in his voice made it even rougher than normal. "And he's good at his job."

"It must mean a lot to you."

He regarded her in silence, then glanced down as he swirled the whiskey around in the bottle.

Angela watched the motion. "How did she die?"

He looked up sharply, eyes narrowed, mouth hard. "I thought you knew she had a heart defect."

"Yes. But everyone thought it was minor. Everyone ... when she was living with us ... thought it wasn't serious."

"Everyone doesn't always know."

"Did Serita know?" she asked before the presumption of the question could stop her.

"You should've asked her."

"I never had the chance."

His expression was enigmatic, but it held some sort of warning. He let out a harsh breath. "What difference does it make now?"

"I just...wanted to know...if she knew. If maybe she..."

"Maybe she what? Knew it? Ignored it? Took chances? Maybe she killed herself? Maybe you want to rake up all the stories the reporters had such a good time with when she died?"

She stared at him, taken aback by the sudden, swift anger, and the edge of violence in his voice.

"I wasn't thinking about the news media."

"No?" The tone was cynical.

"No," she shot back at him, angered herself. "It's not something I think about as a matter of course. It's one of those things you don't have to concern yourself with when you sing for a hundred people at a time, in Nebraska, without benefit of a flock of reporters covering your performance and a crowd of groupies hanging around the stage door."

Jesse's eyes narrowed under the brim of the black hat. He leaned a few inches closer to her on the railing, assessing her steadily, his gaze dark, even, brutally perceptive, unsoftened by any civilized veneer of kindly half-truths. "Is that why you're here, Angel?"

Her eyes widened in wary surprise.

"You want to try out the reporters and the groupies? You want to see if you can measure up?"

She didn't answer.

His dark gaze flicked down over her again, the suggestion of double meaning arrogant and unconcealed.

"You want to know if you can fill Serita's moccasins?" The question hung in the air between them, hard as the clean, sharp notes of a lead guitar, half challenge, half invitation.

For a sudden, confusing moment, the challenge and invitation were equally appealing, equally terrifying. The space between them was charged with an electrifying current of emotion.

The flickering lights of the city, spread out beneath them, seemed distant and unreal. Angela's gaze dropped to the solid concrete of the balcony where they stood, then moved slowly up to Jesse's hand-tooled cowboy boots, his worn, snugly fitted jeans, the silver snaps of his black shirt. Her eyes stopped just short of his face. The defensive protest on her lips evaporated, undermined by the substance of a reality she couldn't deny.

"Maybe I'm scared I can't handle Serita's audiences," she told him, the words a little husky.

"Maybe you can't." He pushed himself away from the railing, then turned toward the sliding doors.

He stopped before he pulled the door open and glanced back at her. Slowly, his mouth curved in a half smile that held assessment, masculine interest and a glint of unmistakable approval. "Then again, Angel, maybe you can."

TWO

Jesse Adam Wilson had a way with a song, and the disorderly crowd that had come to hear him knew it. Angela stood in the wings of the stage where she had auditioned for Jesse and Jack O'Malley the day before. Now she listened to Jesse play to a full house, leading the noisy, boisterous crowd as he wished, controlling them as if he were a good revivalist stirring up his congregation. When he sang a slow, sad ballad, his voice rough timbred and intimate, the emotion in the hall quickened as if there were a chemical change in the air. When he launched into a hard-driving, fast-paced dance tune, the crowd picked up the mood and handed it back with interest. Angela could see, in the first rows, the illegal beer cans tipping up. The jostling and joking were losing their restraint. The rowdy, partying atmosphere was building to a rebellious peak that had her instinctively waiting for the calming sentences meant to quiet the mood of a restive audience.

Jesse uttered no such emollients. He knew what he was doing, and did it anyway, feeding the Saturday-night barroom mood with seemingly inexhaustible energy. She could only admire his skill, despite her apprehension about what he was doing to this crowd.

Gil Hackett, the long-haired blond roadie who had helped set up the concert and now stood beside her in the wings, whistled and stamped at the end of each song as loudly as any of the fans. He grinned at Angela in response to her glance, gave a thumbs-up sign, and stated, "They're hot tonight, huh?"

She acknowledged the inarguable fact with a terse nod. They *were* hot. They took cues from each other with the ease of veteran musicians, seemingly hearing one beat, one rhythm, without conscious notice. Hank Martin set a solid bass line that was reinforced by Carlos Riverra's drums and the driving beat of Jesse's guitar. The harmony was picked up by Tony Almot, the rhythm guitarist, a man of Jesse's age and vintage, who'd been playing with him for ten years. Like Jesse, he wore cowboy hat and boots, claimed no respect for conventional law and order, and seemed to draw some sort of excitement from the fact that this crowd was on the edge of control.

Angela bit her lip, imagining what it would be like to walk out onto the stage in front of this audience and sing for them. The thought brought a twinge of panic. On the tour, she would open the performances, so she wouldn't be expected to *follow* this act. But even the challenge of singing for a crowd that had come to hear Jesse, expecting to be whipped up into this mood, made her throat dry and her hands shaky. She was no stranger to stage fright. No performer was. But this dread was something more than she'd had to contend with in the past.

Jesse moved into a down-and-out country-blues tune and the crowd quieted, listening. She could feel their reaction: the almost palpable sense of increased heartbeat, sexual energy raised another level. It was the reaction he'd intended to get; she knew that. But there was nothing calculated in the raw emotion he projected from the stage. It was real, and she felt her own response as if she'd been sitting in the front row. A ripple of excitement touched her stomach, and an ache of emotion formed in the back of her throat.

The song was familiar from one of his earlier recordings. The words were about loss and longing, and the heartbreak and vulnerability Jesse conveyed were as sensual as anything she'd ever heard before. He sang through the verses, his rough voice testimony to the message of the song, then he replaced the last line of words with the plaintive notes of a blues guitar. The riff was picked up by Tony Almot, then traded between them, building in complexity, mood, the universals of loneliness and human longing, until Jesse, through with it, nodded to Frank West to take up the lead on his fiddle while Jesse stepped back.

Angela, caught up in the music, let it flow through her. Her body swayed in unconscious movement, and her head was tipped back, her eyes half closed.

Jesse glanced toward the wings. He gazed at her for an instant, then he nodded, flipped his guitar strap over his shoulder and set the instrument down on a stand at the back of the stage. He walked toward the wings, leaving the band playing.

Angela straightened, self-consciously pushing her hands into her pockets as she watched his purposeful approach. She hadn't intended to be noticed.

The magnetism of that tall, lean body, the broad shoulders, the easy grace of movement was disturbingly sensual. He'd unbuttoned the first two buttons of his blue chambray shirt, and he unfastened another one as he crossed the stage. When he stopped in front of her she had to pull her gaze from that open collar to look up at his face.

"Want to join us, Angel?"

"What?"

He shrugged one shoulder toward the band. "Play a couple of tunes with us. Whatever you want."

"I—no, I—" She shook her head quickly. A wave of panic rose in her throat.

Jesse's eyes narrowed. "Be an easy way to get your feet wet."

She glanced toward the band on stage, then back to Jesse, and shook her head again. "No."

"Scared, Angel?" There was an edge to his voice.

Angela swallowed. "Look, I don't do the same kind of music." She gestured toward the stage with one nervous hand, palm up. "That's not my style. I don't do that kind of thing."

"We'll do whatever you want. We're pretty versatile."

She shook her head.

Jesse's mouth curved cynically. "You *are* scared."

She pushed her hands into the pockets of her jeans, and hunched her shoulders inside her Jesse Adam Wilson T-shirt, willing her heart to slow its pounding. At the open collar of Jesse's shirt she could see a faint pulse beating in the hollow of his throat, compelling and sensual, like his voice. With an effort of will that reflected years of disciplined practice, she made herself look up at him again. "No. I sing alone. My own material. I don't sing with a band."

The black eyes met hers in cool evaluation, then he shrugged, turned, and walked back on stage.

Angela caught Gil's sidelong disapproval before he glanced away. She pulled her hands out of her pockets, slowly, her face hot.

It was true: her material wouldn't mesh with Jesse's band. It was also true that she was scared of this audience, and of what Jesse did to them.

There was a rumble of clapping, stomping and whistling as Jesse picked up his guitar and started the intro to his latest hit, an ironic composite of double entendre and invitation called, "Make Me Love You Tonight." In the first row, a western-shirted cowboy had lifted his girlfriend onto his shoulders, and the girl applauded spiritedly as Tony Almot grinned at her from the stage. She lost balance, laughed, and clutched at her boyfriend's neck. Her tank top slipped off one shoulder, sacrificing whatever claims to modesty it had ever possessed, and some of the men around her cheered and whistled. Tony leered before he turned toward Jesse and picked up the guitar lead.

Angela watched the exchange without comment, her panic subsiding slowly as her heart returned to its normal rhythm. She glanced toward the soundboard a few rows into the hall, where Tony's wife, Nancy, worked the sound mix. Angela had spent the afternoon working with her, rehearsing for her own future performances.

Nancy Almot was a pro, like the rest of them. Extremely good at what she did, she was tanned, hard-bitten, cynical, and more than tolerant of the kind of rowdy attitude this crowd was working up to. She'd learned sound mixing because she wanted to keep an eye on her husband, she'd told Angela with straightforward candor. "When a Texas man goes out on the town, you got to expect him to come home with more than just an evening's memories, honey," she'd stated. "I make sure what he comes home with is me." She'd kept up the comments all afternoon. "No problem with the mix," she'd said at the end of the session. "You sound real good."

Angela looked down at her Jesse Adam Wilson T-shirt, then glanced back to its prototype on stage. This afternoon she'd been satisfied with what she sounded like. Now, listening to Jesse and the band, she felt again the self-doubt she'd carried with her since she'd been hired. He was good. He was reckless, wild, and irresponsible with the power he held, but he got away with it because he was good, and this rowdy audience knew it.

The song ended. Jesse took off his guitar and stepped to the microphone. He waited, uncharacteristically, for the applause to die. Into the impatient pause he said, "I'd like to introduce a lady who's going on tour with us in a couple of weeks."

Angela looked up sharply. Her heart lurched in alarm. Onstage, Jesse adjusted the mike, making it lower and leaning down to talk into it, glancing toward the wings. Angela's mouth dropped open in shock. "She wants the stage to herself, so we're all gonna go have a beer and listen to her."

There was a spattering of untidy applause and a moment of vague confusion as the band members glanced at each other, put down their instruments and straggled off the stage. Hank Martin, setting down his bass, gave her a wide grin across the stage, but Angela stood where she was, silenced by disbelief, her feet fixed to the floor. Gil Hackett glanced across at her, then bent down and got her guitar out of the case, stood up and held it out toward her.

"Here you go," he prompted. "You can plug into Jesse's amp. The monitor will be right in front of you."

She took the guitar, let out a breath of stunned, lightning fast preparation, and walked out onstage.

There was more scattered applause, a murmur of speculation and a few whistles. Her knees were unsteady as she stopped in front of the microphone, swung her guitar over her shoulder and made a minor adjustment to the mike stand. "Thank you," she said into the mike. Her voice rasped in her throat. She swallowed hard. She could sense the mood of the hall: willingness to be entertained mixed with dissatisfaction at Jesse's exit. They would give her half a moment's grace, then she would have to give them back something they wanted to hear. Something that sounded like Jesse Wilson. Or—maybe closer to the truth—something that sounded like Serita Black.

She strummed a chord on the guitar, checking the tuning, trying to ignore the fact that her throat was closed and dry, her fingers felt as stiff as cardboard, and she was

dressed like a groupie, in ancient jeans and Jesse Wilson
T-shirt. She forced herself to make eye contact with two or
three faces in the audience and searched for some connection with the mood she sensed in this hall. A beer can caught
her eye as it tipped up in the front row, and wry, desperate
inspiration struck her.

With a barely managed smile, she hit the first chord of an
up-tempo ballad about moonshining and dodging the law in
Tennessee.

There was an unexpected, shrill, hillbilly yell, and it was
echoed in a few corners of the hall. Nancy Almot turned up
the volume just enough to make Angela's voice and single
guitar carry over the background of this audience, enough
to make the contrast with Jesse's band dramatic and effec-
tive. Angela sang the number through, every word audible,
and when she finished the song there was a wave of genuine
applause. It didn't match the response they'd given Jesse,
she knew that, but it was real, and it was approving.

Angela let out a breath, and muttered, "Thank you."
Then, without waiting for silence, strummed another chord.
She was experienced enough to know she had to build on
this crowd's approval, and she had a sense, from listening
to Jesse, of what they wanted to hear.

She strummed the notes of an old, cheatin'-heart lament
she'd listened to on the radio as a child. She sang it the way
she'd heard Kitty Clint sing it a hundred times, with a catch
in her throat that spoke of a hard life and working-class
troubles.

Again, when she finished, there was applause, this time
mixed with a few whistles and a little stomping.

She could have them. The idea shot through her with a
thrill of elation that held, with the excitement, a strange
element of fear. *She could do it.* She knew dozens of
moonshiners' songs and broken-heart blues tunes. She could
give them something they wanted to hear. If not her own
songs, then something she'd heard other singers do. She

could feel the response. They were half-willing, on Jesse's testimonial, to listen to her, and make her the focus of their emotions—to accept her as the replacement for Serita.

A sudden, momentary picture of her dead cousin as she must have stood on this stage, red-painted nails gripped around this microphone, brought a disorienting shock of panic and a sobering jolt of comparison.

She wasn't Serita. She couldn't compete with that vivid, vibrant image.

Angela quickly gasped a rush of breath that felt as if she'd been punched and her own hand, with its short, unpolished nails, closed around the mike stand hard enough to feel the slick surface of the metal. The last of the applause was dying out, the sound tentative, hopeful, the audience waiting for her to continue.

She glanced toward the wings where Jesse was slouched at the side of the curtain. There was a self-satisfied, I-told-you-so smile on his face. He nodded at her, raised one hand in front of his chest, thumb and forefinger touching. Apparently she'd passed Jesse's test. On his terms. On terms dictated by his audience. At a time of his choosing.

A surge of anger flooded through her, erasing the panicked disorientation. Well, all right. She'd proved herself. She didn't have to prove anything more. She didn't have to fill Serita's moccasins. Angela turned back to the audience. "Thank you," she said, and walked abruptly toward the wings, leaving behind a blank silence broken by a few questioning murmurs.

Jesse met her halfway to the curtain and slipped his arm around her waist to stop her. It took her enough by surprise that she made no protest when he brought his hand up under her chin, tipped her face up, and kissed her, casually, arrogantly, and with a sense of showmanship that was born of long, stagewise experience. Catcalls and whistles pattered in from the hall. He lifted his head but let his fingers rest on her cheek for a moment before he dropped his arm, turned, and sauntered to the microphone.

He threw a lazy smile toward her as she made her way to the curtain. "Thanks, Angel," he muttered into the microphone.

The sexy implication was unmistakable, and the audience responded as expected, with applause, whistles and shouted suggestions. Jesse grinned at them, struck a chord, and went into his act.

He was good, all right. Talented and smooth and sexy. And as ruthless as anyone she'd ever met in this ruthless business.

Gil Hackett glanced at her a moment, then reached for the guitar she held in a grip tight enough to imbed the marks of the strings in her palm, and said, "I'll take that, Angela."

She let go of it.

"You sounded great," he told her.

She smiled at him. "Thanks."

"They really liked you. So did Jesse."

Angela's smile disappeared in one swift stroke as she turned back to the stage. Gil put her guitar away with no further comment.

An hour later, when Jesse had finished the last encore and left the stage, she'd honed her anger to a fine edge, and Jesse's grin did nothing to take the edge off.

He ambled toward her, pushing his cowboy hat to the back of his head.

"You were just fine, Angel. You sounded like you could be the first folksinger to make it really big at the Grand Ole Opry."

"I know what I sound like." Her voice was cold.

Jesse's smile disappeared. "Yeah, I suppose you do."

Gil Hackett gave them a quick glance, then picked up the amplifier nearest the curtain and carried it out the stage door.

Angela's angry gaze didn't move from Jesse. "I didn't appreciate being railroaded into that performance."

Hank Martin, walking up behind her, interrupted them, draping an arm around her shoulders and grinning at her. "Not bad, An-ge-la." He took in Jesse's half-sour smirk, and Angela's tight-lipped expression, then moved tactfully. His lips pursed in a silent whistle. He nodded to Jesse and left.

Jesse watched him out. "Yeah," he said again, to Angela. He pushed his hands into his jeans pockets. "Well, it went fine, didn't it?"

"That's not the point! You had no right to make me go on without warning, Jesse."

He looked her in the eye and said, as if it were the unadorned truth, "Y'had warning. I asked you if you wanted to play with the band, and you said you'd rather go on alone."

"I know what I said," she snapped. "And that wasn't it!"

"Look, you got no call to be so fired up about it. You did just fine out there. You did better than just fine, as a matter of fact."

"Better than you expected?"

"That's not what I said. And it's not what I meant. And it's not like it's the first time you've been in front of a microphone, Angel."

"It's not the first time you've been in front of one either. What makes you think it gives you the right to play God?"

Jesse Adam Wilson returned her angry glare, then, deliberately, lowered the brim of his hat. "All right, I didn't give you much choice about going on when you didn't want to." He waved an arm in a movement that indicated his contempt for the backstage wings. "All you wanted to do was stand out here and wonder if you had what it takes, and then stew about it for two weeks until we start the tour."

"What business is that of yours?"

"This tour is my business."

Outrage gathered in her chest. "I wasn't about to cancel out on the tour. You didn't have to worry about me losing my nerve."

"To tell the truth, Angel, you didn't have much left to lose."

"That's not—"

"It *is* true, and you know it."

"I wasn't ready, dammit! You had no right."

"You never would've been ready. You don't 'get ready' to work an audience like that. You just go out and do it whatever way feels right. You throw yourself into it and go with the mood, Angel. You don't stand around 'getting ready'."

"I don't work like that. I don't do a performance as if it were some kind of party."

"Y'did it, didn't you?"

"Well it wasn't my kind of music! It's not my—that's not the way I work. I'm not—" She broke off, hands raised in front of her in a gesture of frustration and anger, then drew in another sharp breath and glared at him.

There was a measure of tense silence. "Okay," Jesse said finally. His voice hardened. "You work your own way. Do it any way you please. But you do it. We've got a tour coming up that needs an opening act, and I want to make sure it has one."

She forced herself not to step back from his overwhelmingly physical presence and the intense force of will it represented. "You don't stop at much to get what you want, do you?" she said bitterly.

He looked at her, silent, tacitly acknowledging the truth of her accusation.

"You're afraid Serita's concert won't get rebooked without me?"

"Yeah, maybe I am." He pushed his hands into his pockets. "That's part of it."

"Well, then, why don't you keep things a little calmer?" she asked, on an impulse of outrage. "Why do you get the crowd so worked up, like it's at some sort of drunken brawl?"

"That's my style, Angel." He stared at her, weight slung on one hip, his gaze steady and arrogant and unwilling to give an inch. "You don't like it, you can listen to someone else."

The voice held stubborn conviction, and the same blatant sexual magnetism that was an unmistakable part of his physical presence. Angela felt it in her own response, immediate and strong despite her outrage. It was, she knew, part of his style, part of what made him so good, along with the huge talent she'd admired since she was twelve, and admired even more now.

She met his gaze and swallowed hard. "I can't say I don't like it," she told him honestly. Her voice sounded almost as rough as Jesse's, and she could feel a pulse in the side of her neck that must be visible with every heartbeat.

Jesse slowly pushed his hat back on his head. Slowly, presumptuously, the satisfied Texas smile crept up his face. "You just got something against partyin', huh?"

"Maybe I just have something against drunken brawls, Jesse. Did you consider that?"

He leaned a little closer and smiled with a little more satisfaction. "You like... *private* parties, Angel?"

She clamped her mouth shut and bent down to close her guitar case. There was a finger-threatening ping as the lock closed. She stood up. "I don't like private parties that include an audience of five thousand or so."

She got two steps toward the door before his Texas drawl caught up with her. "Think you'd like to try it without the audience, Angel?"

Her shoulders stiffened as another roadie walked by wearing a couple of electric cords and a barely concealed smirk. She took one more step and spun around again.

"What would you call that? A rehearsal to make sure you got it right on stage?" Her fists clenched at her sides. "I don't think you need any rehearsals for that. You really put on a professional show. It was a great *act*, Jesse!"

There was a gratifying silence from Jesse Adam Wilson. She held his surprised gaze for a second, then, with grim satisfaction, turned again toward the stage door.

"Angel." He raised his voice to carry through the back-stage wings. "You were good."

The words stopped her in her tracks as if he'd flung a lariat and she was the rodeo calf. He strolled up behind her and waited for her to turn around.

When she did, there was a faint smile on his lips. His dark gaze drifted down over her shirt and worn jeans. Then he looked back up to see her slightly parted lips and the green eyes that held, behind her defiance and her anger, transparent doubts and the vulnerable, undeniable need for Jesse Adam Wilson's approval.

"You were damn good," he said softly.

She felt a breath go out of her lungs in a shaky sigh that undermined her anger and left her with a confusing sense of reaction. Jesse Adam Wilson was a consummate artist, whose judgement of her music held the power of unquestioned predominance. But he was also a man who made her pulse beat faster and her stomach tighten in physical response. She had to swallow again before she found the voice to mutter, "Thanks."

"I figured you would be."

Angela looked at the floor, then shook her head in brief, modest denial. Her moment of panic in front of the microphone flashed back to her, charged with the vibrant image of Serita in feathers and beads, dazzling her audience wherever she played.

"You could really be something. You know that?" he said.

She didn't know it, she realized. When she compared herself to Serita, she lost the ability to judge herself or her potential. After a few seconds she looked up, then stared out toward the stage, now half-darkened and busy with the hustle of packing up.

Jesse's gaze followed hers. He frowned and looked back at her.

"Nancy did a great job," she said quietly, a little awkward. "With the mix."

"Yeah, she did. She knows the hall."

"You've played here before?"

"Once. About a year and a half ago." He glanced toward the stage again. "It was a sellout. We went an hour overtime on the show, and Rita brought the house down on 'Crazy Love.' Then we went out on the town to celebrate." He looked out toward the dim expanse behind the closed curtain and his eyes narrowed. She had the eerie feeling he could see the same vision she herself had pictured when she was out there. Serita with her hand clasped around the mike stand, black hair catching the multicolored reflections from the spotlight. "We must've hit half the after-hours joints in Dallas," Jesse continued. "And I think they probably all remembered us."

"I can guess that wouldn't be too hard."

"No, it wouldn't." He gave her his familiar grin and hooked his thumbs in the pockets of his jeans. The look turned assessing. "Want to go someplace and have a beer?" he asked suddenly.

She shook her head tersely, staring at him.

"No?"

"I'm not much of a drinker."

"Come on, Angel." There was a note of urgency there that sounded, disturbingly, truer than the cynicism. "You just sang for the biggest crowd you've ever been in front of. What are you going to do. Go back to your room and drink orange juice?"

"Yes."

He let out a harsh, disbelieving chuckle.

"That's what I do after performances. I go back to my room, get out my guitar, play a few songs and go to bed."

"Alone?"

"Yes."

The maroon velvet curtain behind Jesse swayed slightly as someone walked by. There was the sound of a heavy electrical cord being dragged across the backstage floor. Jesse pulled a hand out of his pocket, let his gaze travel down the length of her figure again, then muttered, "Suit yourself, then. *Angel.*"

An unexpected sense of Serita's memory—a puzzle with pieces missing—flashed into her mind. "Are you going to hit half the after-hours joints in Dallas?" she asked him.

He gave her a long, enigmatic stare, then glanced out at the stage again before he looked back at her. "Well I'm sure as hell not going up to my room to drink tea." He spun on his heel and picked up his guitar.

The stage door closed behind him on a sudden, sharp silence, an unfinished confrontation, and a flutter of eagle feathers hanging from the handle of the guitar case.

Three

The road sign read Welcome to Waco, in ten-inch black letters that reflected the midmorning sunlight with brash Texas belligerence. Jesse Wilson, stretched out on a couch in the lounge section of the tour bus, peered at it through the tinted glass window and automatically calculated the distance to their next scheduled stop. Fifteen miles.

Across the carpeted floor, Frank West dealt out one more hand of gin rummy. The TV squawked over the drone of the bus. Nancy Almot was listening to the CD player, wearing a set of headphones. There were several sets available, but Jesse wasn't tempted to listen. He'd heard all Nancy's favorite show tunes before.

"Hey, Jesse!" Hank Martin looked up from the desultory card game in the corner. "You got five bucks I can borrow?"

Jesse reached into his pocket for his wallet. A name and phone number scribbled on crinkled motel notepaper fell into his lap when he pulled out the money. He glanced at it as he folded a five-dollar bill and paper-airplaned it toward Hank, then held up the crinkled memo in Hank's direction. "Who did you say this was from?"

Hank shrugged. "Don't know. The desk clerk just handed it to me. Didn't say where it came from. I don't read your mail."

Jesse frowned at the small square of paper with the motel logo at the top. The places where they stayed while on tour weren't kept secret, but they weren't advertised, either.

The number had a South Dakota area code. "Call Red" was the only message. Jesse didn't know anybody, as far as he could recall, named "Red." He straightened the crease in the middle of the note, stared at it for a few seconds more, then hitched himself up on the couch. He reached in front of Tony Almot for the radio-controlled phone, steadying it as the bus bumped over a gully in the highway.

The call was picked up on the third ring. "CJ Auto Parts," a voice answered.

"Jesse Adam Wilson. I want to talk to Red."

"You got him, man."

There was something too slick about the voice. Jesse felt a prickle of dislike in the back of his neck, irritating because it had no logical cause. "I got a message to call you," he said.

"Yeah, man."

Jesse didn't fill the subsequent silence.

"I got a business proposition for you," the voice interjected.

"What kind?" Jesse said finally.

There was a snicker. "Profitable."

The dislike crystallized into aversion. "You do a lot of business at out-of-the-way motels in Texas?" Jesse asked shortly.

"I do business all over the world. And right now I got a buyer who's interested in...ah...Indian artifacts. The kind that once belonged to Serita."

Jesse felt a muscle clench in his jaw.

"I could cut you in fifty percent on whatever you sell. We're talking big money, man."

"There's nothing for sale. *Man.*" There was a dangerous edge to his voice. Beside him, he saw Tony glance over, eyebrows raised.

"You haven't heard the price yet. My buyer is a serious... uh, collector."

"Why don't you dig her up? Maybe you could sell the pieces."

"Hey, no need to get upset about it, man. I had as much respect for the lady as you. But business is business—"

His hand tightened around the receiver until the knuckles showed white. "I don't do business with the kind of slime that crawls out from under a rock. Why don't you—"

He stopped. The line had gone dead. Nancy was looking at him with apprehension that matched Tony's. Hank's gaze skittered away when Jesse glared at all of them. The expressions were made by friends who knew him better than to make comment.

With a sudden, harsh oath, he stood up and flung the phone against the couch cushions.

Tony, retrieving the phone, muttered a low, "What the hell?" as Jesse stalked into the front part of the bus and slammed the door behind him.

Angel glanced up and turned her head at the sound. She was sitting by herself in one of the upholstered seats, two rows behind the driver's compartment. He'd forgotten, in his brief outburst, that Angel was here.

He stopped, in front of the door, meeting her eyes for a moment in cool evaluation. Then he scowled, strode down the aisle, and took the seat across from her. He folded his arms over his chest.

She gave him two seconds further observation, then turned back to a notepad propped on her lap.

He glanced across at her. The letter she was writing was half-finished. Her head was bent over her work. One small, long-fingered hand held a corner of the paper while the pen formed private words. Smooth, ash blond hair fell in a loose curtain in front of her face.

"Breakfast coming up," he said, after a moment.

The wide mouth gave him a brief, neutral smile. "Sounds good. I'm starving."

She went back to her letter, politely granting him privacy that he realized, half-surprised, he didn't want.

"Who's this one to?" he asked.

She looked up. "My grandmother."

"Thought you wrote to her yesterday."

"That was my aunt."

"Thought your aunt was the day before yesterday."

"My sister."

Jesse adjusted his hat, and his mouth quirked. The bus slowed to turn off the highway to the roadside restaurant where they'd scheduled a stop. He pulled himself up from the seat, then leaned down to stare out the window.

Standing in the aisle, he could see past Angel's shoulder to the sheet of white stationery propped on its box. *Dear Gramma,* the heading started. Like a kid writing a letter home from camp. Feelings of disbelief, impatience and slow amusement flickered through him. The only other person he knew in this business who wrote letters was his lawyer.

Everybody else did their work over the phone. He felt his jaw tighten at the reminder.

He stared at the sheet of paper covered with Angel Trent's neat, rounded handwriting, then met her startled gaze as she looked up over her shoulder and caught him. The expression in the wide, innocent, smoky green eyes touched him with a small jolt, like the smooth surprise of good Kentucky whiskey. He felt his physical response, instantaneous and powerful.

Unconsciously he straightened a little more, and his gaze fixed on her face. He'd felt the same reaction two weeks ago when he'd walked in on her audition and heard her sing. It had taken him by surprise then, too.

The Angel's face was like her voice: clean, innocent, but with a cadence of suggested sensuality underneath the innocence. Her skin was like fresh cream, like the elusive beauty found on a Victorian cameo. She made him think of keeping secrets, of private passion behind closed doors, of something held back....

She gave him a sarcastic smile that didn't touch the innocence in the eyes. "Do you want to read the rest of it?"

Disoriented, he glanced at the letter, then looked back at her. The bus had pulled to a stop. He touched two fingers to the brim of his hat, nodded, and muttered, "Just waiting for you, ma'am." He watched her slide out of the seat. When she bent forward her jeans were pulled taut over the trim backside.

There was a lot to be said, he decided, a slow smile curving his mouth, for lust.

From the separate driver's compartment Gil Hackett emerged, rubbing his fingers over his eyes. He glanced from Angel's distant smile to Jesse's half leer, grinned knowingly, then swung the bus door open. He walked toward the rear lounge. "Pit stop!" he called. The rest of the band members straggled out of the lounge door as Jesse and Angel followed Gil out to the parking lot.

Nancy Almot gave Angel a vague, bleary-eyed smile as she stepped out into the sunlight, making a show of being hung over. She was playing it a lot worse than it was, he knew. "There ought to be a law against someone that can look like you do first thing in the morning, honey," she grumbled at Angel, then looped her arm through Carlos Riverra's and muttered, "C'mon, sweetheart, lead me to the coffee."

Angel grinned and shook her head good-naturedly at Nancy's words. Jesse offered Angel his arm, but she merely tipped her chin toward him as her grin changed to a polite smile, pushed her hands into the pockets of her parka and headed toward the restaurant. He shrugged and followed after her, his eyes on the threadbare patches on the backside of her jeans. Apparently he hadn't made a big hit yet with the Angel. Then again, maybe the way she ignored him was a clue. She was just holding back.

He smiled wryly, but that didn't quite change the speculation in his eyes. He'd watched her perform onstage for three nights now, and he had the sure knowledge that she was holding back. Her performances were competent, careful and professional. The voice, like the face, was as clear and true as springwater, but the spark of potential he sensed in her talent was missing. She kept all raw emotion under wraps. What she could do if she let loose was anyone's guess. He grinned. He seemed to be spending a lot of time making guesses.

But then, there was a lot to be said for lust.

For one thing, it was a lot better than the chill of repulsion he'd felt when he was on the phone to some unknown sleaze who'd thought he would sell Serita's relics. His hand unconsciously closed into a fist at the recollection of that oily voice.

The cynical grin faded. They were going to do Rita's benefit concert. Nothing in hell or heaven was going to stop it.

He took a long step and reached in front of Angel to hold the door open for her. She gave him another quick smile, innocent and polite, then walked in.

The diner was small, clean, a little shabby, the atmosphere supplied by the smell of strong coffee and grilled bacon. Jesse slid onto a booth beside Carlos and Nancy, across from Angel and Gil. The rest of the band and Jack O'Malley took the booth behind them.

A plump, middle-aged waitress with frizzed hair and a world-wise set to her mouth approached with a coffeepot. She looked them over as she poured their cups, made a quick character evaluation, and focused on Angel. "What'll it be, honey?"

Angel gave her a wide smile and an order for scrambled eggs, toast and orange juice.

He might have guessed that the Angel would believe in a good breakfast, along with letter writing, clean living and general good manners. He slouched back in the booth, letting his gaze drift over the cameo of her face, giving his imagination free rein.

"Pancakes and sausage," Gil told the waitress when she looked at him.

Nancy groaned and covered her eyes with one hand. "You mean I'm gonna have to watch y'all eat?"

Jesse smirked at her, then glanced up at the waitress. "Two eggs over easy, hash browns, sausage and toast. And bring some catsup."

"Lord, Jesse," Nancy grumbled.

"Just coffee, honey?" the waitress asked her blandly. Nancy nodded. The woman scribbled on her pad, stuck it into her apron pocket, and sidled comfortably toward the kitchen, calling out the orders to the cook as she went.

Nancy moved her hand away from her face and eyed them all with familiar morning-after accusation. "You-all had as many beers as I did," she told them. "Except for Angel."

"That's our Angel," Jesse commented.

The gray-green glance flicked toward him. Her expression was ironic, but she said nothing.

"I don't know, honey," Nancy told her. "This morning I think you've got the right idea."

"But you always change your mind, Nance," Jesse put in, grinning. "Can't resist a bottle of good beer." The grin uncurled as his gaze moved back to the green eyes and innocent face. "Unlike the Angel, here, who can resist anything."

"Even you, Jess?" Nancy snorted, then nodded at Angel. "Keep it up, honey. No reason to make it easy for them."

Angel smiled sweetly. "And sometimes there's no reason to make it at all."

Jesse smirked at her in silent difference of opinion, while Nancy laughed again.

With a squeak of protesting hinges, the restaurant door swung open and Hank Martin hurried through it, exuberant and bellowing. "Hey, listen to this, boys and girls!" He was carrying half a dozen copies of a top music magazine, the top copy open to the rock and country reviews.

He tossed a copy to Jack on his way past his booth, then slid in beside Angel and grinned irrepressibly at her. "They love us again," he announced. "Listen to this. 'The Jesse Adam Wilson Band's new tour proves they've lost none of the hard-driving beat or sharp-edged musicality that propelled them to the top of the charts ten years ago.'"

"All right," Gil crowed.

"'Sharp-edged musicality'?" Carlos repeated, pained.

"'Appropriately restrained was their recent tendency toward animalistic antics on stage.'" He scanned down the page while Jesse let out a sarcastic whistle and Carlos snorted in disbelief. "Here we go, Angel. 'Some of the credit for the welcome change in style must go to talented newcomer Angela Trent, the blond beauty who opened the evening—'" Hank broke off to leer at her.

Angel stared back, eyes wide with surprise. Two dashes of pink appeared in her cheeks. She reached for her own copy of the magazine.

Hank went on reading random phrases. "'Purest soprano on the C&W circuit . . . honest ethnic authenticity of material and approach . . . the Jesse Wilson Band is back on track with this tour. . . .'" He grinned again at Angel, then dropped one edge of the page to wrap one arm around her shoulders, pull her toward him and kiss her enthusiastically.

Jesse's hand, reaching for a copy of the review, halted halfway across the table. He stared at them as an old feeling, born of masculine hormones and familiar since puberty, coursed through him. Nancy raised her eyebrows and gave him a sidelong glance.

He scowled at her and snatched a copy of the magazine out from under Hank's elbow, as Angel pulled away, chuckling, and shrugged off the bass player's arm.

As Hank had said, the reviewer loved them. And loved the Angel. That was the basic message, packaged in the usual media double-talk. Predictably, there was a long, semipsychological analysis of Serita's influence, musical and otherwise, of Angel's relationship to her, and the inevitable conclusions and comparisons. They couldn't leave it alone, he thought cynically.

Though Angela Trent doesn't deliver any of Serita Black's fire and fury, the contrast in its own way carries a message to the musical community that bears interesting analysis. The post-Serita Jesse Wilson delivers enough fire of his own....

Jesse grimaced, dropping the magazine on the seat beside him. He gave Hank a sour look and shoved his hat farther down on his head.

The waitress returned with their orders and distributed the plates around the table, then nodded to Hank, waitress pad in hand. "What'll you have?"

He glanced up from the review. "Beer. Draft."

She nodded without even a flicker of surprise, started to turn back to the kitchen, then hesitated, peering around at them with curiosity and dawning recognition.

They all recognized the look. A general air of well-worn resignation stopped conversation. Everyone stared at the table.

"Say," the waitress began, "aren't you...aren't you Jesse Adam Wilson?"

Jesse gave her a slight grin, tipped his hat, and picked up his fork.

"Well, I'll be." She beamed at them. "Imagine that."

There were halfhearted smiles around the table while the food cooled and they waited, impatiently polite, for the waitress to leave.

Hank shot a hopeful look toward the bar, but the waitress didn't move. "My daughter listens to you all the time," she gushed, with a wide smile. "She's a real fan."

"That's great, ma'am," Jesse told her.

"Wait'll I tell her you were in here. She won't believe it. She must have all your records," the woman continued. "Her baby keeps her up all time—poor little thing has colic—and when she gets to crying and won't stop, her mama just puts on one of your records and turns it up real loud to cover the crying and walks her back and forth."

Hank covered his eyes with one hand and disguised the movement as scratching his forehead.

Jesse smiled at her again. "Nice to know we have a purpose in someone's life."

"Oh, well, I—I didn't mean it quite like that—" The waitress, now flustered, hovered in the aisle beside the booth, her order pad in hand. "She's always been a fan of yours," the woman hurried on. "She was even saving up for a black hat, but she spent the money on baby clothes. She don't have much money. See, her husband just up and left."

There was silence around the table. The waitress paused, glanced at the barely tolerant expressions, then shrugged awkwardly and muttered an embarrassed, "Well, you folks don't want to hear about that, and here I am, running off at the mouth."

Angel put in, with quick sympathy, "What's the baby's name?"

Carlos glanced at Angel, sighed, and put his napkin back on the table.

"Jessica. Jessica Ann Lawson. She's named after her mama."

"It's a pretty name." Angela smiled, breaking the awkward constraint.

The waitress fidgeted with her order pad, then glanced at Jesse, clearly torn between wanting an autograph and the fear of imposing.

Hank cleared his throat and looked toward the bar.

The waitress jumped guiltily. "Well, here I am keeping y'all from eating. I'll bring your beer right away," she told Hank.

"Ma'am?" Jesse's query stopped her as she turned. He took off his hat, gave it a long appraisal, then held it out to her across the table. "For your daughter," he said.

"Well!" The woman hesitated, startled, then beamed as she took it. "Well, thank you," she said incredulously. "Well, I'll be. Jesse Adam Wilson's hat. She'll be so excited. I do thank you."

"My pleasure, ma'am." He nodded to her, lifted two fingers to the hat brim no longer in place, then picked up his fork and gave her a quick grin.

The waitress left them all staring at Jesse with mixed surprise and disbelief. He glanced around at them in silence, then looked down at his plate. "Pass the catsup, Nance," he muttered.

Angel was letting her eggs get cold, eyes on Jesse, when he looked up at her. She quickly glanced at the magazine on the table.

"Like it?" he asked her testily.

A faint wash of color crept into her face, but she looked up at him and held his gaze. "Yes."

Hank gave her an easy grin. "First time you've been reviewed in this rag?" he asked her.

"Uh-huh."

"Well, it's official, An-ge-la. They say you're good."

She turned back to catch the edge of Jesse's hard stare. "You don't need reviews to know you're good," he told her.

She didn't answer.

"Or to know what you do to an audience. *You* know what you can do."

She watched him a moment longer, then she shrugged. "It's worth something to hear it in a review."

Jesse nodded. "Yeah, it's worth something." He folded up the paper and rolled it into a tube. "Hey, Jack," he called over his shoulder. "Why don't you get on the phone and make some calls?"

He tossed the rolled paper toward the next booth. Jack O'Malley caught it, one-handed, just before it landed in his order of pancakes.

"Tell 'em about us bein' appropriately restrained," Jesse said.

Jack set the paper beside his plate and grimaced. "I'll handle the phone calls, Jess. You handle the restraint."

Half an hour later Jesse followed the members of his band as they straggled onto the bus. Most of them made their way back to the lounge. A TV talk show blared for a moment, then the sound was cut off as someone plugged in a set of headphones. Jesse stood in the aisle behind Angel as he watched her pick up her unfinished letter and slide into the seat. He leaned toward her.

"This seat taken, ma'am?" he asked.

She looked up in surprise, shook her head politely. "No." As Jesse slid in beside her, she folded her letter and put it into the side flap under the window. A curtain of straight, silky hair brushed forward, the color halfway between brown and pale gold, subtle and varicolored as the west Texas prairie grass. Jesse's eyes lingered on it when she turned toward him, pushed the hair out of her face and leaned against the window.

He didn't bother to disguise his interest, but she didn't respond to it. The bus idled to life and pulled out of the parking lot onto the highway, growling rhythmically as it worked through its gears. Dappled light from the window glinted on Angela's hair. The self-composed face had a serene beauty that held some sort of elusive fascination for Jesse.

"That was a nice thing to do, in the restaurant," she said, still leaning against the window. "To give your hat to the waitress."

He shrugged. "It's just a hat. You can buy them all over Texas."

"You don't have another one with you?"

He glanced up, then ran his fingers through his hair, dropped his hand and hooked his thumbs in the pockets of his jeans, settling into the seat. "Never figured I needed more than one hat. I only have one head."

She smiled. In the backlighting from the tinted glass, Jesse could see the faint laugh lines at the corners of the wide gray-green eyes. They barely kept her from looking like a sixteen-year-old. Jesse's gaze dropped momentarily to her mouth.

The mouth could have been sweet sixteen.

"You ever been married, Angel?" he asked abruptly.

Her eyebrows rose, and she shook her head. "No. If you're about to ask, 'What are you waiting for?' you can move to another seat."

"I wasn't about to ask. I'd much rather speculate about it."

She crossed her arms. Her cotton sweater pulled taut against her breasts. "It's not that unusual," she said shortly. "And I haven't had that much time."

"You've had twenty-six years."

She gave him a sharp glance. Her chin was tilted at an obstinate angle. "Have *you* ever been married, Jesse?"

"Yeah. I have."

Sudden surprise showed on the expressive face. Jesse's mouth curved slightly. "Seventeen years ago," he said. "I guess it was before your time. The publicity folks didn't make much of it, especially after they got hold of Rita."

There was a pause. The growl of the engine rose a notch as the bus pulled into the passing lane. "No," she said. "I didn't know about it."

"It didn't last long. She didn't like being on the road. I didn't like staying home."

"You must have been pretty young."

"Eighteen." He gave her a faint, outlaw grin. "But I still don't like staying home."

She returned his gaze silently. The green eyes were level, a little wary, and there were barely visible freckles across the bridge of her nose. Her mouth was quirked slightly, as if to keep in all unwarranted emotions. *Holding back.*

The thought brought a quick, curious tightness to his stomach.

"Then maybe you'd better not get married again," she said finally.

"Don't have any immediate plans to."

The sweet-sixteen mouth smiled ironically.

Jesse's eyes perused her mouth with lazy interest. "I might be talked into fooling around a little...." he told her.

"That wasn't a proposition, Jesse."

"It wasn't? Well, maybe I'll just speculate for a while about what it was."

She shook her head. The ash-blond hair shimmered on her shoulders. "You don't quit, do you?"

"No, I don't."

She sighed then faced dismissively forward and leaned over to readjust the papers she'd stashed in the side pocket. Her hand paused for a moment on the copy of the magazine review before she pushed it farther down.

"Going to send the review home to Gramma?"

"No." The tone was self-composed.

"Why not? It's innocent enough. Won't dirty up your squeaky-clean reputation."

"I don't think my grandmother's worried about my reputation."

"Who is, then? You?"

"Me?" Her eyebrows rose in the beginning of a reaction to his goading. "What does that mean?"

He gestured at the magazine. "The critics may love you, Angel, and for once they know a good thing when they hear it. But *I* think you could give them a lot more than 'authentic ethnic roots.'"

Her back stiffened visibly. The slight smile was replaced by a stubborn, resentful set of her mouth. "I'm not trying to give anybody 'authentic ethnic roots,'" she said belligerently. "That's what I sing. I am authentic."

"Maybe so, Angel, but if you dish out much more ethnic purity you can set yourself up as a professional Prairieland virgin."

"I'm a folksinger." She snapped at him with a sudden, swift flare of temper. Her eyes glinted with enraged sparks. "Not a rock star. If you want glitz, you'll have to find someone else. And if you want the kind of publicity you got with Serita, I can't oblige you on that either." There were two spots of angry color in her cheeks. She glared at him, her self-possession vanished in the heat of a vehemence he hadn't quite expected.

He fell still for a moment, eyes narrowed, assessing her outburst.

A harsh breath lifted her breasts against the cotton sweater. "I'm not superstar material, Jesse. I'm afraid I can't compete with that." She turned sharply toward the window, propped her elbow on the window ledge and jammed her fingers into the hair at the nape of her neck.

He waited for her to look back at him. When she did he gave her a grim smile. "Is that what's holding you back?

Serita? How'd the review put it? You don't have her 'fire and fury.'"

She stared at him.

"You're afraid you won't measure up to your cousin."

The wide mouth thinned against a flare of defensive anger that was all the more telling by contrast to her usual composure. "There isn't anything holding me back," she said vehemently.

"No?"

"No!"

"You don't care how you stack up against Rita in the newsmagazines?"

"No, I don't."

"You don't walk out on stage and wonder if anybody's thinking about rock stars?"

"I'm a folksinger. I'm not—"

"That's bull, Angel." He appraised her as he propped one boot on the edge of the seat and rested his elbow on his knee. "As they say in West Texas. I don't how they put it in East Nebraska."

"Well, *I* know how they put it in East Nebraska. And I know what they like to hear in East Nebraska. And that's what I sing."

He leaned closer to her. His knee brushed her arm and she pulled back as if she'd been burned. Jesse's eyes flicked to the sleeve of her sweater, where he'd touched her, then met her smoky gaze again.

"You could do better," he told her. "You're a hell of a lot better than that cream-of-wheat stuff you've been dishing out. You could do some of your own material. Or some arrangements with the band. Why don't you take a few chances on it?"

"I do take chances! Walking out on stage and singing folk music in front of the kind of audiences who come to your— *events*, is taking chances enough to qualify anybody as a damn fool where I come from!"

Jesse was silent. He watched the play of emotions on her face and saw resentment, anger and defensiveness, mixed with something vulnerable enough to prick his conscience. But there was a hint of unleashed passion that drew him like a desert wanderer to a watering hole, and wouldn't let him back off.

"That's what you hired me for!" she burst out, when he didn't answer her. "Why are you pushing it?" Her eyes were dark with the emotion she'd been keeping rigidly controlled. The look she gave him was passionate and unguarded.

His gaze moved down, to her slightly parted lips, then to her breasts. He slid his foot off the seat. "Maybe I just want to see what you'd do if you weren't holding yourself back, Angel."

There was a faint, indrawn breath, a wary, unconsciously defensive movement of her hand. "I'm . . . not Serita," she said, the words breathy.

"So who says you have to be?"

Her gaze dropped, then flicked tellingly toward the magazine in the side pocket.

"The music critics."

She looked back at him.

"It's written in a magazine so that makes it God's truth?"

"It makes it true for a lot of people. I don't presume to know about God."

"Well, I know something about the truth: you don't get it from the critics."

She stared back at him, her elbow still propped on the window ledge, her hand threading slowly into her hair again.

"You a regular reader, Angel?" he asked with a flash of sudden perception.

"Yes."

"Well, it was a hell of a poor way to find out about your cousin."

The light from the window dappled as they passed an overhead bridge. Silence stretched out between them.

"You mean none of it's the truth?" she asked finally.

"None of what?"

She gave a self-conscious shrug. "The parties. The—drugs. That you and Serita were...a couple."

"We were once lovers." She reacted to the word with a slight flare of color in her cheeks. "I don't guess you could say we were a couple."

Jesse watched her, his eyes serious. She swallowed down whatever reply she might have made. She wanted to ask him, he sensed, about the parties and the drugs.

"She didn't have much of a childhood, growing up on that reservation," he said, before she could speak. "You know that, I guess. No money, no future anybody could see, nothing you could ever call a family."

"I—I know."

"She made her own family. Made her own laws." He turned his head to face forward and sighed. "I got a phone call this morning. Some bastard that wants to buy Rita's eagle feathers and sell 'em as high-priced souvenirs."

"Sell them?" The tone held shock and distaste. He recognized the feeling as an echo of his own.

"All the Indian...paraphernalia," he went on. "It *meant* something. Something more than money. She made it mean something. No matter what else..." He looked at the roof of the bus, focusing on nothing specific. "She had a wild streak.... She used whatever she could get to prove—something."

At his waist, his fingers toyed absently with the Navaho-designed, silver-and-turquoise belt looped into his jeans. Before he realized what he was doing, glanced down at it, and let out another long breath.

"That was hers, wasn't it?" Angel asked. "The belt?"

"Yeah. For a while. She won it in a poker game, off a guy named Luke Standing Horse. On the reservation." He moved his hand away from the buckle. "I won it off her later. With a straight flush." He gave a huff of laughter. "It took a straight flush to win against Rita. And then you didn't always know whether you'd really won."

"I always knew she'd make it." The words were softly spoken, but with a shading of conviction that made them more than wistful sentiment.

Jesse's gaze flicked toward her.

"I knew she'd do anything she had to, to make it. As if she had nothing to lose." She gazed back at him, eyes wide. "The music, singing, was all that mattered. She could go on a stage and give everything she had with nothing left over for herself."

"And that's the way you see it? You have to keep something left over for yourself?"

"It's not the same! I'm not that kind of singer. I don't perform that way, and I don't live that kind of life—and I'm not Serita." The vehemence in her voice trailed off on the last word, fading into an uncertainty that was at odds with her natural confidence. Jesse's gaze played over her face.

"What kind of life?" he asked.

The flash of defensive anger returned to her eyes. "The kind of life that has all that pressure. The kind of life where the wrong choices seem like the ones to make. Being on the road all the time, not having any family, not having a home. The crowds and the publicity and the unreality. I don't want that."

Jesse's mouth curved in cynical contradiction. "For someone who doesn't want it, Angel, you're a hell of a long way from Nebraska."

She flashed a defiant glance at him. "I'm here because I want to find out about my cousin."

"You think that'll make you happy? Finding out?"

"Was *she*? Happy?"

"I can't answer that."

"Why not?"

"She's dead, Angel," he said bluntly. "You can't bring her back. You can spend all your time worrying about what she was like and whether she was happy, and if you could ever take her place." He leaned toward her, his shoulder a fraction of an inch from hers. "Or you can go out on that stage and find out what you can do yourself."

"I know what I can do myself. I'm a folksinger."

Her gaze faltered in the face of his hard stare.

"If that's what you want to settle for, Angel."

She turned toward the window without meeting his eyes.

There was a span of silence, filled by the rumble of the engine and the steady hiss of the tires on the road. "Suit yourself," Jesse said. The words had a contemptuous edge, even to his own ears.

The innocent face looked back at him, the smoky eyes vulnerable, troubled—full of the emotion she kept so carefully under wraps.

"On second thought, I take that back," he told her. He leaned across the seat, supporting himself with one hand on the back of it, then reached for her face and turned her chin toward him.

He brought his mouth down on hers with deliberate, demanding pressure. It was a kiss born of old frustrations, old, unresolved anger and some hard, unexamined urge to push her beyond her cautious, self-imposed limits.

The startled childlike sound she made altered his purposeful onslaught beyond any conscious intention. His mouth softened, and his fingers, gripping her chin, loosened their hold to touch her with what was more caress than command. His thumb brushed her throat, while on her soft, as yet unresisting mouth, his lips moved slowly, seductively back and forth.

Her breath felt warm as her lips parted, then opened under his. Surprised by the response, the touch of a tongue, his own sudden, swift arousal, he moved his hand around to the back of her neck and threaded his fingers into her hair as he slid closer to her and brought his hand around her back to pull her against him.

She pushed away, one hand against his arm, and turned her head to the side.

His fingers stayed at the back of her neck an insistent moment longer, then he let them trail over her shoulder as he pulled his arm back and slouched in the seat.

She leaned against the window, putting a few more inches between them. Her mouth curved in a quick, strained smile. "I haven't made out in the back seat of a moving vehicle since I was in high school." A breathy chuckle escaped her throat.

She darted another look at him, then shook her head, the gesture as jerky and uncertain as her words. "I—don't think it's my style."

He smiled slowly, and he leaned toward her. "We could try it again, just to make sure."

She hesitated.

When she finally looked up at him, her gaze was wide, wary, vulnerable as a child's.

Jesse's cynical smile faded, leaving in its wake a vague, disturbing, itch-under-the-skin sense of violation. For the second time in the space of a morning, he was amazed at his own emotions. He let out a bemused chuckle.

"Tell me one thing, Angel."

"What?"

"You're not in point of fact an original Prairieland virgin."

She looked away at the empty seats across the aisle as she covered the lower half of her face with her hand. When she dropped her arm to her lap, there was a slight, ironic smile on her wide mouth. "I'm not a virgin, Prairieland or otherwise."

"Good." He slid out of the seat and stood in the aisle, one hand on the plush upholstery. "I was afraid I might've just done something that would get me sent straight to hell."

He nodded at her taken-aback expression, ran his fingers through his hair and headed toward the lounge.

There were hats, among other things, for sale in Waco, he told himself.

Black ones.

Four

Angela hooked her stocking feet on the rung of a backstage stool in the wings of the Lubbock, Texas Memorial
Auditorium. She watched the sound crew readjust another
amp and set another monitor, following Jesse's instructions. The crew had spent the past two hours moving
equipment onto the stage. They were having trouble with the
balance, and her own sound check would have to wait until
Jesse was satisfied with the electronics. No one expected that
to happen anytime soon.

Her guitar was on her lap. She propped it up and
strummed the intro to an old Carter Family tune she intended to use as her opening to the night's performance,
then muted the strings with an impatient hand and shifted
restlessly on the stool.

"A little more bass, Nancy," Jesse called out, his voice
echoing in the empty auditorium.

"I just cut it back!" she protested.

"Well, turn it up!"

Angela played the guitar intro again. Dissatisfied, she changed a chord in the progression, then fished a flat pick out of her back pocket and tried the intro Carter-style. The new progression didn't please her any more than the one she'd been playing for years.

When it had sounded fine.

She let out another sigh that ended in a sour smile. It was nerves, pure and simple, and the impact of Jesse's critical demands. She knew how this music was supposed to sound. "If it's not broke, don't fix it," her grandmother liked to say. She should stop trying to fix it.

Jesse barked another order to the sound crew.

In spite of herself, Angela strummed the intro again, changing another chord, playing it at a different tempo, listening evaluatively. The change gave the melody overtones of...Texas swing, she decided. But the flavor was a little wrong. She tried again, making the chord a seventh. It worked, she realized, surprised. With a minor change in the rhythm it would be even better.

"Hey, sounds good, An-ge-la."

She looked up.

Hank Martin grinned at her. "Ha yew?" he asked.

She smiled back at him and gave him the standard Texas reply: "I'm fine. Ha yew?"

"I like that bass run. You got a good thing there."

She shrugged. "I was just fooling around with it."

"Play it again."

The easy grin was engaging and convincing. She glanced at him and played the progression again.

"Yeah, nice. You ought to try it with bass and drums."

The guitar echoed as she shifted it in her lap. She considered the idea, then shook her head. "I'll work on it some more."

Onstage, Jesse called out instructions for another change, and one of the roadies obediently dragged a monitor to the other side of the mike.

Hank grinned at Angela. "Unless Jesse gets finished with the sound setup, it won't matter how much you work on it. We won't ever get to play. You been waitin' here all afternoon?"

She nodded.

"Someone should've told you it would take 'em a while. You could've gone out for lunch without missin' a thing."

She smiled ruefully. "I must be missing something all right. I can't figure out what they're doing out there. It sounded fine to me an hour ago."

"Yeah." He nodded. "Sounds fine ain't words you hear a lot in this band. Jesse don't like to settle for sounds fine."

She glanced down at her guitar. Her mouth curved in an ironic smile. "I know."

He assessed her for a moment. "Yeah. Everybody that works with Jesse knows." He reached behind a curtain. "Have a beer." He offered her a can, then reached back for another.

She gazed at the can for a moment in surprise. Her mouth quirked wryly at what she knew was Hank's version of a picnic lunch, then she let out a half-disbelieving laugh and took it. "Thanks." She took a polite sip, her eyes on Hank over the rim of the can. "How long have you been working with him?"

"Five years."

She lowered the can slowly to the edge of her stool, her eyes watching Hank, her expression reflective. "Before Serita joined the band."

"Yeah." He drank from his beer, then slanted her a look. "Before Rita."

There was an awkward beat of silence. Angela tipped her head down toward her guitar, fingering the strings.

"Get that damn reverb out of the voice mike, Nance!" Jesse hollered.

Angel looked up at Hank and said, her voice carefully casual, "Was she as demanding as Jesse?"

Hank's eyebrows rose for an instant in puzzled, blank response, and Angela added, "About sound checks?"

"Well, no..." He gave a single shake of his head, lips pursed. "No, Rita never cared much for sound checks." He drank again, then glanced toward Angela and let out a soft breath. "Sometimes, toward the end there, she didn't even show up."

Angela frowned. "I thought that was a house rule. Everyone has to be here for sound checks."

"Yeah, well." He shrugged and glanced down at his beer. "Rita got away with more than most of us."

"Oh?"

Hank drank again. He wasn't, she realized, going to explain.

"Why was that?" she asked with sudden aggressiveness. "Because she was so good? Good enough to get away with breaking the rules?"

He looked at her and shook his head, lips pursed again. "I wouldn't have used the word good, exactly."

Angela kept her eyes fixed on him. Her eyebrows were drawn together in a frown.

He lifted his beer, started to ignore her, then stopped before he took the drink and leaned toward her. He said, making a point, "She got away with it because most everybody in this band is a *man*, honey. Particularly Jesse."

"Oh." She felt a shimmer of uneasy emotion that she couldn't explain. The question, Was he in love with her? hovered on the tip of her tongue, wanting to be asked. Abruptly she slid off the stool to place the can of beer on the floor, then sat again, her guitar in her hands. Her fingers toyed with the strings.

"Play that riff you were workin' on," Hank suggested. "I liked that."

She gave him a brief smile and complied.

"Yeah. Sounds good. You gonna use it tonight?"

She shook her head. "I think I'll stick with what I know."

He grinned. "Crowd control?"

"That's what I was hired for, isn't it?"

There was an edge to her voice, but Hank didn't seem bothered by it. He merely nodded, agreeing with her. "Yeah. You've been doin' a good job of it, too. You're makin' Jack real happy."

Her smile flickered ruefully. Whatever she'd been hired for, she wasn't making Jesse happy. She wished she could shake the feeling of inadequacy that fact brought.

Onstage, Jesse called out, "Frank! Try the fiddle." From the opposite end of the wings, Frank appeared, fiddle in hand, in front of the microphone.

Angela put her guitar down flat in her lap. "Do you think the benefit concert will be rescheduled?" she asked Hank.

"Jesse wants it real bad. And he usually gits what he wants." He glanced out toward the stage. "Sooner or later."

Her glance followed his, toward Jesse. "But not from Serita," she said. The edge was back in her voice, sharper than she'd intended it.

Hank's gaze met hers and skittered away. " 'Cept Rita," he echoed.

She waited for him to say more. Instead, he drained his beer, then crushed the can and tossed it toward a trash barrel behind the curtain. Onstage, Tony picked up his guitar and started chording to Frank's fiddle lead. Music filled the auditorium.

"Why didn't she show up at sound checks?" Angel said, over the volume of the music. "She cared so much about singing—about her career."

Hank shrugged evasively, then reached behind the curtain for another beer. Angela's eyes didn't move from his face while he opened it, then looked up. He shrugged again. "Hell, Angel, I don't know. She was hung over, or—somethin'. Rita liked to party."

"So does Jesse. But he's never too hung over to do a sound check."

"I know that." He repeated the shrug, then said awkwardly, "They didn't always party...together, An-ge-la."

"You mean she dated other men." It was a flat statement, but the note of uncertainty must have been audible even over the music.

Hank frowned, clearly taken aback by her probing. "Well, there was a guy up on the reservation, for one...." He shook his head, then gave a cynical, wry grin. "Hell. She did whatever she pleased. Weren't nobody could stop her."

"Stop her from what?"

Hank didn't answer her.

"Seeing other men? Partying? Being hung over?"

His gaze slid away from her face.

Angel's suspicions jelled into a cold mass in the pit of her stomach. "Using drugs?"

Hank drew the fingers of one hand over his cheeks and along his jawline. He looked back at her. "It's not that uncommon, Angel. You must have known." He assessed her face for a moment, his eyebrows raised. Then he muttered, "No, I guess not." He stared down at his feet, grimacing. "Maybe I shouldn't'a mentioned it."

"She was my cousin." Her voice was so tight it was barely audible over the sound in the hall, but her face, she knew, carried the message. "I have a right to know," she said more forcefully.

"Maybe so, Angel, but—"

"It was covered up, wasn't it? For the newspapers and magazines."

Hank turned toward her, leaning one shoulder against the stage support. Over his shoulder she could see Jesse walking toward them, but her attention was focused on Hank, her words accusing. "When did she start?"

Hank drew in a sharp breath. Angela kept her demanding gaze pinned on his face. "I don't know," he said. "She wasn't into it much at first. She just liked to go out and party and have a good time. She drank a lot, but—"

Jesse was within arm's reach before Angel glanced up at him. She was unprepared for the action when he reached around Hank's slouched body, wrenched the beer can out of his hands and flung it toward the trash can. Beer sprayed out from the top of the can in a steady stream, and the can hit the barrel, bounced off it, and clattered onto the floor, accompanied by Hank's shocked, "What the hell!"

Hank turned an astounded gaze at Jesse. Perplexity and growing anger marked his face. "What the hell, man?"

Jesse jammed his hands into his back pockets. The seams strained as his fists bunched inside the worn material. "Conversation's over, Martin. Get your butt out there."

"Well, it's a hell of a way to ask!"

Jesse jerked his head toward the stage, his mouth tight with controlled anger. "This is a sound check. Not some sort of a backstage gossip party."

"Yeah, I know what it is!" Hank stared back. "I been waitin' around here for two hours."

"And you found a way to fill in the time, didn't you?"

"Yeah, I did. What of it? All I was sayin' was—"

"And *I'm* saying shut up about Rita."

"Why?" The question was Angel's. Both heads snapped around toward her. She glared at Jesse. "Why is it such a closed subject?"

"Because I don't want to talk about it."

"And nobody else is supposed to talk about it, either?"

"You got it."

"Did she O.D.? Is that how she died?"

His eyes seemed to bore into her. The force of his anger made her heart race with an answering rush of adrenaline, but she stared back at him fiercely, refusing to back down.

He gave Hank a swift, warning glare that made him take a step back, palms raised, and turn toward the stage. Jesse's black gaze moved back to Angel. "Yeah," he spat out viciously. "She died of an overdose."

The cold lump in Angel's stomach rose to her throat. She swallowed convulsively.

"Does it make you happy to know that?"

"No, it doesn't! But—"

"Does it satisfy you, then? Now that the truth is out? Or do you think you want to spread it around a little more?" His voice was scathing. "Maybe you'll have to advertise it."

She stared at him while silence stretched out between them, taut and unnerving, and her heart thudded in her chest like a trip-hammer. In the half-darkened theater discreet noises attested to the presence of a dozen uninvited, intensely interested witnesses.

Finally, without speaking again, Jesse spun on his heel and headed for the stage door. It squeaked on its hinges, then banged shut, the sound startling in the unnatural quiet. Angel let out a shaky breath and her shoulders slumped, as the steel formed by anger ebbed out of her backbone.

The click of Nancy's high-heeled cowboy boots broke the silence. Nancy stopped in front of the curtain, hands on her hips, resigned, while her gaze moved from Angel's face to the spilled beer can. "Well," she said prosaically, "I guess somebody's got to clean this up." She looked around her. "Anybody got a rag?"

"I'll take care of it, Nance." Angel felt the reassuring pressure of a hand on her shoulder. Jack O'Malley smiled at Angel, managing a matter-of-fact tone with professional ease. "Take a break, Angela," he told her. "Twenty minutes, while Nancy sets up the sound on Hank, then she'll do yours, okay? You want a cup of coffee?"

She shook her head and smiled perfunctorily.

He nodded, gave her another reassuring smile, and turned back to the stage. "You plugged in, Hank? Ready?" At the bass player's curt nod, Jack turned back to the hall. "Okay, let's get back to work. We've got a performance tonight."

Crisis assuaged, the business of staging a concert went on.

* * *

It was close to midnight when Angel let herself into her hotel room, set her guitar down in the carpeted entranceway, and slumped back against the door she'd closed behind her. She leaned against the wooden panels for a moment, eyes closed, then pushed herself upright and toed off her half-laced boots. In her stocking feet, she walked across the room and dropped onto one of the twin beds. The hand-knitted afghan she brought with her everywhere was tossed carelessly at the foot of the bed. Its bright splash of color contrasted with the off-white bedspread. She reached for a corner to pull the wrinkles out, and her hand unconsciously stroked the wool even after she'd smoothed the folds.

The sound mix had been perfect.

The concert had gone fine.

No one in this tight, professional crew had slipped up just because a beer can had been flung across a stage floor in violent anger and the star had walked out. He had appeared again, three minutes before his set, and had gone onstage with the kind of frenzied energy that had the audience stomping and whistling and calling for more. The rift between Jesse and his bass player might never have happened. The charged emotions that Angel had fought down to do her own performance seemed, in Jesse, to channel themselves naturally into the energy of his music. She'd found herself watching him, as mesmerized as any of the star-struck groupies in the front row. She was as eager as they were to believe the intimate need in the rough voice, the promise of love and commitment that a long, cold look at his life-style could have told them he wasn't about to offer.

Some of them would have settled for a one-night stand. Jesse, no doubt, knew that.

Angel had left before he'd seen her, packing up her own guitar and making her way back to the hotel by herself. She

wasn't one of those who would settle. Jesse didn't need to
know how well she understood the temptation.

She gave the afghan another tug, and reached for the
phone to dial room service.

Tea was on its way, the kitchen assured her.

She got up and headed for the bathroom, reaching behind her neck to undo the loop and button of her flowered,
western-style silk dress. The high-necked collar drooped
forward slightly as she undid a few more buttons.

There was a knock on the door as she was rinsing her face
and groping for a towel.

"Just a minute!" she called out. Towel in hand, she
crossed the room to pull the door open. With the same
movement she leaned over her guitar and pushed it out of
the way.

When she looked up, Jesse Wilson was standing in the
doorway, one boot crossed in front of the other, weight on
one hip, a hand stuck in his pocket. In his free hand he held
a mandolin case.

"Oh." It was all she could say. She stood, clutching the
towel, for a stunned, silent moment before she got out, "I
thought . . . you were room service."

A smile curved one corner of his mouth. "You going to
send me back?" He pushed his hat farther up on his head.
He'd changed from the denim jacket he'd worn all afternoon and through the concert. Now he had on a pale yellow embroidered cowboy shirt, tucked into the ragged
waistband of his jeans. The vee of skin beneath the open
collar was damp, and he smelled of the hotel's soap.

A tiny thrill of panic, like an echo of the emotion she'd
felt that afternoon, sent a shiver from her knees to her
throat. The thought of the front-row groupies flashed into
her mind and brought a flush to her face. When she moved
to open the door wider, she was stiffly conscious of her
body.

Jesse walked in past her. The mandolin case looked incongruously small against his thigh. She'd never seen him with anything but the eagle-feather-adorned guitar. He jiggled the case idly while his gaze roved around the hotel walls and furnishings, taking in Angel's few personal belongings in the bland, off-white room. When he turned toward her his gaze paused for a few seconds on the towel, still clutched to her chest. Abruptly he met her eyes. "I guess you expect an apology."

The sudden directness of his gaze was unsettling. She crossed her arms in front of her midsection, towel still dangling from her hand, and gave him a quick, disconcerted smile. "It's not necessary."

The intense black gaze didn't waver. "I don't know if it's necessary or not, but for what it's worth—" Without taking his eyes from hers, he reached up and tipped his hat. "I'm sorry, ma'am."

"That's—quite all right."

She watched his mouth curve in a grin that made a slight crease in one cheek. In the side lighting from the room, he looked the way he had on the jacket of an album she'd bought four years ago: intense, enigmatic, sensual. There was a tightening in her stomach that had nothing to do with echoed emotion, that was directly, sensually related to the present moment.

He swung the mandolin a little toward her. "I thought you'd be playing your guitar, drinking tea."

"The tea's coming."

"Oh, yeah. Room service." There was another short silence. "Mind if I join you?"

"No, I guess not." She uncrossed her arms, waved the damp towel toward the phone, and asked, "Do you want something besides tea?"

He shrugged. His mouth curved again, slowly. "How about some music?"

She laughed, then gave a small, awkward shrug and said, "All right."

Jesse crossed the room to put his mandolin case on one of the twin beds.

As soon as his back was turned, she tossed the towel into the bathroom. It caught on the corner of the sink and hung there, precariously balanced, like her own unstable emotions. She left it hanging and got her guitar, then sat on the bed opposite Jesse, watching him take out his mandolin, loop the strap over his shoulder, try the strings. The instrument was old, of dark-stained wood, with intricately curved body and ornate inlay. Jesse adjusted a peg and strummed a chord. In the carpeted hotel room, the high, bell-like tones were muted but still clear.

The small instrument held against his chest emphasized his broad shoulders and muscled forearms. His head was bent over the fret board. Black, unruly hair, a little too long, not quite as straight as she had once thought it was, curled behind his ear, under the hat. His hands, sensitive and strong on the steel strings, held the instrument with sensuousness that could have belonged to a lover.

He glanced up and caught her gaze, and she felt heat rising on her neck.

"It—has a beautiful sound," she said before he could give her that friend-of-the-devil smile. "You don't play it much anymore in concert."

"No, not much anymore." He glanced down at the instrument. "I got her back east. New York. But she's a Texan now. All that Texas music." When he looked up, the slow, sexy outlaw's grin tugged at the corners of his mouth.

She felt its effects all the way down to her toes. "My uncle plays the mandolin," she said. "I've always liked it."

Jesse strummed another chord. "Your whole family play music?"

"Just my uncle." She watched his fingers moving on the fret board. The mother-of-pearl inlay under the strings was worn in the same way as the markings on her uncle's well-used mandolin. The childhood memory of that old, familiar instrument crossed her mind like an unexpected visitor, unexpectedly well remembered. "He was Serita's father," she said. Her cousin's name stuck in her throat, but speaking it seemed to release some of her tension.

Jesse looked up at her, a flicker of surprise in his eyes. "Rita's father played the mandolin?"

She nodded. "Traditional music, mostly. A few fiddle tunes. When he was younger he worked a night or two at the Grange dances."

Jesse smiled speculatively. He played a few random notes, checking the tuning, then asked abruptly, "How'd he get mixed up with an Indian woman?"

"He was in the army. Stationed near the reservation."

He played a few more notes. "From what I heard about Rita's mother, she didn't seem like the type to fall for a Nebraska farm boy."

Angel met his gaze, her eyes steady and candid. "From what I understand, she got pregnant. So they got married."

"Did the right thing, did he?"

"I think he tried."

Jesse gave her a long, assessing look, his expression still speculative. "Yeah, I guess that's the only thing someone in your family could do."

She blinked, taken aback by the answer, but Jesse's glance was on the mandolin again, his fingers moving on the strings. He started a melody, soft and clear, familiar.

The high, rich-toned, repeated notes of the mandolin carried the tune as if it were sung. She could almost hear the words: Down in the valley, the valley so low... Her hands, on her own guitar, filled in the chords automatically.

There was a knock on the door. She stopped playing.

Jesse's head turned briefly toward the sound, but he kept on with the melody while she put her guitar down on the afghan, got up, and went to answer it.

The music of the single instrument followed her across the room. *Hear the wind blow, dear, hear the wind blow*...

In the hallway was a uniformed teenager holding a tray. He peered into the room, listening, craning his neck for a look at Jesse, before Angel handed him his tip and closed the door on his still curious expression.

Hang your head over, hear the wind blow... She poured herself a cup of Earl Grey, self-conscious about her partly unbuttoned collar as she leaned over the desk, her back to Jesse. The melody didn't falter, but she heard the creak of bedsprings as he shifted his weight.

He was leaning against the headboard, boots propped up on the white spread, when she brought her cup back and sat on the other twin bed.

Jesse's eyes followed her, then he started to sing, crooning the familiar words about love in a rough, low voice. "Roses love sun...shine, violets love dew. Angels in hea...ven know I love you."

He looked up at her, the mandolin cradled in his hands, the dark gaze resting on her face, the expression half smiling. Her hand, setting the cup on the night table, stopped moving.

"Know I love you, dear, know I love you..."

Oh, he was good, Angela thought. He was more than good. He was a mesmerizing Texas drifter with a voice that was magical. It could weave a spell that put butterflies in her stomach and made the words sound as if no one had ever said them before. No matter how often she'd heard them.

She hadn't heard them like this....

As if in defense against her feelings, she put the cup down and reached for her guitar. The chords of the accompaniment came without conscious thought, but she didn't trust her own voice to sing, even when Jesse left a verse open for her.

When the song ended, his gaze stayed on her face while the half smile turned into the slow, familiar, outlaw's grin. "You don't know the words to that one, Angel?"

"I can't sing it like you do."

He picked out another run on the mandolin, still grinning. "Sing one for me."

"What . . . do you want to hear?"

"Sing one you wrote yourself."

She smiled in what could have been acquiescence, but when she started to play, it was a well-known, traditional ballad.

He let her finish it, embellishing the melody as she played, not joining in the words. When it was done, he let the music trail off, watching her reflectively. "You didn't write that."

"I haven't written anything as good as that."

"I don't think that's the point."

Angel shrugged. "I don't always feel like doing my own music."

"Not even on request?"

"No."

He started playing once more, idly picking out a thread of music. His dark gaze drifted slowly down to her feet, then back up again. "That dress is . . . nice," he told her. "Suits you."

She felt warmth in her cheeks.

"You're supposed to say thank-you."

"Oh," she said, the tone wry.

"And you're supposed to play one of your songs when it's requested."

The subtle provocation could almost have been imaginary, but to her acutely sensitive nerves it carried unmistakable challenge. It gave her an edge to resist the electricity, and she wasn't fool enough to let it go by. She took a deep breath and made her voice sarcastic. "If your purpose is gentlemanly seduction, Jesse, you shouldn't be pushing the point."

He sucked in one cheek. "I guess gentlemanly seduction ain't my style." He gave her another appraising look, and another desperado's grin. "That dress must've looked great onstage. All the little buttons up the back. Must've had every male in the place wonderin' how it comes off."

"I think that's an exaggeration."

The suggestion of melody went on, idle but evocative. "I didn't catch your performance tonight."

"You wouldn't have liked it any better than the others. I'm still a folksinger."

He grinned again, but the shading was a little darker than his mood of a moment ago. "Oh . . . yeah. A bastion of traditional heartland values." The grin dissolved into the harsh lines of some emotion darker than the cynicism she'd gotten used to. "Always live by the rules. Try to do the right thing. Except sometimes that isn't enough, is it?" The melody stopped. He appraised her in the sudden quiet. When he spoke again, his words were knowledgeable, and there was a suggestion of challenge in the tone. "Sometimes a nice young Nebraska farm boy accidentally fathers some little half-breed who just won't fit into any of the slots. Your heartland values don't give you any answers for that one. Do they, Angel?"

She stared at him, her eyes wide, a quick rush of offended outrage stiffening her back. "You have the answers, then?"

"No." His hand, clasped around the neck of the mandolin, tightened convulsively before he loosened the grip and looked up at her. The trained voice was strangely raw when he spoke. "I did what I could to stop her, Angel. She knew I wouldn't have any drugs in the band—onstage or in the bus. But I couldn't do anything about the times she was off on her own."

There was a strain in the words that told her what they had cost him to say, but she couldn't afford to recognize it. Her own emotions were too volatile, too tangled, too close to release.

She clasped her guitar against her midsection as if it could keep in the feelings and summoned up a defensive anger as a protection.

"Oh, no," she said bitterly. "All *you* could do was cover it up after she died." She knew the accusation was unfair, but it was flung out in some response to the unfairness of Serita's death. It hung suspended between them, unwarranted, angry, divisive.

"Yeah," he said harshly. "Yeah, it was all I could do, and I did it."

She didn't answer him. Her hands felt damp on her guitar. She swallowed the rest of her unjust censure before she could say it, but her mouth was a straight, mutinous line.

"Rita made a lot mistakes," he went on, still in that strained voice. "But that doesn't change what she did with her talent. She made her mark."

"Is that supposed to make it okay? She made her mark on the world before she checked out?"

"It counts for something. You can't take that away from her. She put her heart and soul into her music. She took every chance she had to, and I admire that more than anything in this world or the next. *Angel.*"

She was silent, her mouth set.

He slid the mandolin strap off his shoulder, put the instrument back in the case, then closed the lid and snapped the catch. He gave her another look and half started to say something more. Instead, he clamped his mouth shut, stood up and turned toward the door.

"Did you love her?"

Her question spun him around. He stayed where he was for a moment, facing her, considering the answer. "Yeah, I suppose I did."

"But Hank said—"

"Hank said what?"

"That she dated other men. The man you talked about, Luke..." Her voice trailed off in puzzlement. Uncertainty replaced the set anger in her face.

"Who she slept with was her business." He glanced away from her, toward the mandolin, and added, "I wasn't one of them, not after the first six months."

"Why not?"

He let out a quick, disbelieving breath at her presumptuous question. Then he swung the mandolin case up onto the bed again, resting it on the mattress and leaning a little toward her. He spoke deliberately. "Because I don't share my women, Angel."

Abruptly, she put the guitar aside, stood up, crossing her arms in front of her midsection. "But I bet you expect them to share you."

His eyes narrowed, then swept down over her in quick, intimate assessment before he met her gaze again. "Is that an accusation, or an expression of personal interest?" There was a faint, wry trace of amusement in the voice; more than a trace of masculine interest in the dark face.

She drew in a quick breath, feeling instant heat in her face. "It wasn't a... personal question."

He pushed back his hat. "I believe most folks would consider a question about their sex lives pretty personal, Angel."

"Most folks don't have a whole row of groupies staring at them nightly with star-struck admiration and heads full of fantasies."

He let the handle of the mandolin case drop, and slowly hooked his thumbs into his belt loops. His eyes didn't leave hers, but his body leaned an inch closer to her. An arrogant grin suggested itself on his face. "Maybe I don't happen to want a whole row of groupies with their heads full of fantasies, Angel."

The back of her knees pressed against the bed. She had no choice but to stand her ground. "I'm sure they'll be disappointed to hear that."

He said nothing for a long moment. Then, slowly, as if he were trying out a well-considered thought, he reached up to trace the curve of her cheek, then the side of her neck and the inner collar of her dress. The back of his knuckle lingered at her throat, where her pulse had started beating in erratic rhythm. He opened his palm and slid his hand around her neck, inside the partially opened row of buttons.

She held her breath, watching him wide-eyed, afraid to move, as if any movement would release the tight bud of emotion in her chest.

He brought his other hand up to circle her neck. Her eyelashes fluttered down as she drew in a shaky breath, and desire gathered in her stomach. His fingers moved on the buttons of her dress, working them loose, one at a time, down her back.

She stood still, unresisting, hypnotized by the touch of his hands on her spine. All thought seemed arrested by the flood of sensation coursing through her.

He stopped when the dress was unbuttoned halfway down her back. He brought his hands up to encircle her neck once again, his thumbs caressing the underside of her jaw.

A shiver of awareness radiated from his hands through her neck and shoulders. As if following it, he slid his palms outward, tracing her collarbone with the heels of his hands, pushing away the unbuttoned dress and the straps of her bra until her shoulders were bare, the dress caught around her upper arms.

"Jesse..." The word was a husky, desperate whisper.

He bent his head toward her shoulder, and she felt the exquisite shock of his warm, wet mouth at the side of her neck. Desire crystallized into something shimmering and powerful, throbbing in all her nerve endings. His hat tumbled off his head as she brought her hand up to thread her fingers into his hair. A small, involuntary sound came from the back of her throat.

Jesse's hands tightened on her shoulders, then slid back to her neck as he tipped her head up and covered her mouth with his. One hand slid down her exposed back, pressing her against him, moving again to the buttons of her dress. His musician's fingers released them dexterously, one at a time, down to the waist, while his lips moved on hers, coaxing them open, seeking admittance.

He stepped back from her a fraction of an inch, the kiss lingering for just an instant before he lifted his head to look down at her, his gaze intent with passion. His palms cupped her face, then brushed down to her neck, traced her shoulders, and slid down her arms, pushing the dress and the straps of her bra down to her elbows. His thumbs hooked on the brief bit of lace and pulled it down from her breasts.

As if his gaze were palpable, her nipples hardened in response to it. She had a sudden image of consummation of this act, and, like an overlay to the imagined picture, a conception of Serita, like this with Jesse, her head thrown back, as it often had been when she sang, her hair spilling down her uncovered back. Angela drew in a sharp breath, then, with a swift, irrational wave of panic, snatched at her dress and pulled it up over her chest.

Jesse stood unmoving, his hands hovering over her shoulders where she'd shaken them off, but his breathing was ragged, and he watched her, shocked, demanding an explanation.

"I—" Her throat felt constricted, as if she could barely force the words out. "I can't—"

He lowered his hands to his sides. She watched his shoulders relax. "Why not?" he said. His voice was gritty.

"Because, I—" The breath came out of her lungs in a rush, and she drew it in again, fighting her own sense of frustration. "Because I'm not—"

Serita's name hung in the air, unspoken, unresolved.

Jesse narrowed his eyes. One corner of his mouth tightened in anger that was darkened by a shade of contempt. "Yeah. You have a real good idea, don't you, of who you're not." He reached for the mandolin, turned on his heel and strode across the room, then let himself out, not looking back at her. The door banged shut behind him.

Angel sank down onto the bed, staring at the door. One slim hand reached toward the afghan, clutching it in her fist. With another sigh, she let her head droop forward and pulled the folds of the afghan around her, wrapping herself in the comfort of its granny squares.

Five

Cow City, Serita had called Amarillo. Jesse gazed through the window of Jack's rented four door while they drove past miles of cattle lots that surrounded the city. In the back seat, Tony and Nancy dozed, ignoring the scenery. The faint, earthy smell of cattle crept in past the car's air conditioner. It was, to Jesse's mind, an improvement on the sanitized, air-conditioned air. He was a Texan, and there was something about feedlots and cattle that appealed to every Texas male; something that spoke of men and horses and end-of-the-trail celebrations.

Something that had nothing to do with wide-eyed, tea-drinking folksingers and panicked, virginal refusals that left a man with enough desperation to batter down a saloon door.

He scowled at the dusty Texas landscape, his thoughts cynical, fueled by frustration that hadn't yet dissipated. He shouldn't have walked away from her. He could have made her forget Serita. He could have ignored her fears. He could have wiped out the innocence in those gray-green eyes...all that defenseless emotion that was as unmarked and as touchable as her skin.

He pushed his hat back on his head, then jerked it forward again.

She was probably in Amarillo by now. The tour bus had left two hours earlier than Jack had, and she'd been on it, headed for the cows and the cowboys.

She could have made *you* forget Serita. The out-of-the-blue, uncanny twist on his thought brought him up short for a moment. He hadn't meant it that way. He frowned, his mouth set.

Her eyes had been wide, vulnerable, reflecting emotions he'd never seen in Serita's. They'd called up emotions in himself that he hadn't felt since long before Serita.

And Angel had brought them out with no seeming effort, the way she did onstage with her clean, expressive voice, and the quality of immediacy that came across even in a timeworn, safe-and-traditional folk song.

Jack drove at a steady pace past feedlots, one after the other, uniformly square and brown, most filled with placid cattle.

Jesse felt a muscle in his jaw tighten.

The last time they'd played in Amarillo, Rita had been with them. When she'd gone onstage, in her feathers and beads, one of the Amarillo cowboys had given an Indian war whoop. Rita had stepped up close to the microphone and given back one of her own—unbridled, hostile, as she'd been at the end, cocaine inspired. "*That's* what it'll sound like, Paleface, when the Comanche rise again," she'd taunted.

A month later she was dead.

And all you could do was cover it up after she died.

Angel's accusation echoed in his mind. There was a sour taste of self-accusation in his mouth. *All you could do.* A judgment from an angel. Who wasn't Serita. Who wouldn't have him.

He could feel a knot forming in his stomach, as convoluted and complex as his thoughts about Angel Trent.

He reached out abruptly to snap the catch on the glove compartment. "You got any whiskey in here?" he asked Jack, his voice gruff.

The question was rhetorical. Jack didn't carry liquor in the cars he drove. They all knew his opinions.

"I'll stop somewhere if you want a soda pop," the manager told him.

From the back seat, Tony gave a derisive snort. There was no comment from Nancy. She was asleep, her head on Tony's shoulder. They'd opted to ride in with Jack so they could take advantage of the later start.

Jesse banged the glove compartment shut and crossed his arms in front of him. "No, thanks." He was riding with Jack because of business. They'd had to make some phone calls. For Jesse, it hadn't been an option.

"Didn't you get your quota of whiskey last night, Jess?" the manager asked, irony in his voice.

Jesse let out a wry huff of breath. "I didn't get my quota of anything last night."

There was a low whistle from the back. "My word. The lady must've turned him down."

Jack's eyes met Tony's in the rearview mirror, then he glanced across the seat at Jesse. "Didn't know you had a lady in Lubbock."

Jesse said nothing.

The manager gave him another glance, sharper than the first. "You don't either, do you?"

He got another silent look.

Jack's hands tightened on the steering wheel. He swore under his breath, softly, viciously, and with the impact of a man unaccustomed to swearing.

Jesse's eyes narrowed, but he met Jack's brief look.

"Tell me," the manager said deliberately, "that it wasn't Angel."

Jesse's silence hung in the air, revealing more than the spoken word.

In the back, Tony started whistling a soft tune, meant to indicate he wasn't listening.

Jack swore again, more explicitly. Anger rose in his voice. "You couldn't leave it at throwing beer across the stage, and telling her what you always insisted she didn't need to know, and insulting her while you were at it. You couldn't leave it at that, huh?"

"Since you seem to think it's your business," Jesse said finally, "you'll be pleased to know I apologized."

"Oh, that makes you a hero. And it's just coincidence that you had to wait until after the performance to do it."

Jesse frowned at him. "Why? Did she have some trouble with the performance?"

"She did fine with the performance. She's done fine with every performance. She's doing a damn good job of a damn near impossible task. And she doesn't need anything else to deal with!"

Jesse's sound of disbelief didn't stop Jack's vehemence.

"She's getting the reviews, the press, the audience response. She's done it with virtually no experience, and, Jesse, you didn't give her any gentle introduction to it, Jesse."

Jesse turned back to the window. "Yeah," he said curtly.

The manager shot him another hard look. "You know the kind of pressure she's under. What the hell do you think you're doing?"

Tony's tuneless whistle took on a note of ironic commentary to the question. It was ignored by the two men in the front.

Jesse crossed his arms. "You think I'm gonna mess up the reviews, Jack?" There was an edge of contempt in his voice.

Jack's broad shoulders tensed in a posture that gave the same message as Jesse's. "I think you're gonna mess up the girl." Hard, stubborn, furious blue eyes met Jesse's. "Give her a break, Jesse."

Jesse returned the glare for a second, his mouth set, then abruptly looked away. Frustrated, he uncrossed his arms to pound one fist softly against the window frame. He turned his head back to the manager. "She's better than what she's been doing," he said, his voice controlled, but with an intensity that drew Jack's sharp glance again. "She's got enough talent to fill up Texas, and she keeps it all wrapped up like she's afraid of it. That tune she did at the audition—the one she wrote—that was the best thing I've heard this year. And she hasn't done it or anything else she wrote since then."

Jack glanced across at him, frowning, taking his turn at silence.

"She could be something this town's never seen before." He leaned toward Jack and propped his arm on the back of the seat, his posture intent, his voice hard with conviction. "She's got more voice, more talent—"

Jack watched him assessingly, his forehead furrowed.

"She could be better than Rita."

The manager's expression sharpened. His eyes met Jesse's for a moment. He said, at last, with slow decision, "What was between you and Rita didn't have much to do with her voice, Jess."

"What's that supposed to mean?"

Jack stared straight ahead. "Angela Trent's been doing exactly what she was hired to do. What she's been doing is a lot of the reason for getting that concert rebooked. You know what's riding on this, Jess."

The air conditioner hummed into the silence.

"Getting that benefit concert scheduled *is* what you want." Jack gave him another look. "Isn't it?"

Without speaking, Jesse turned away. The outskirts of Amarillo moved by them in steady sequence. Cows stood stolidly in the heat. In one of the pens a small herd, bellowing protests, was being driven toward an open gate by a dusty, sweating cowboy who was no doubt thinking about a beer and shower, maybe a night on the town...a woman.

A woman with cornsilk-colored hair, and smoke-green eyes, and skin like new cream. And a whole line of restraints. Like a whole row of tiny buttons up the back of a silk dress.

Jesse could feel Jack's assessment even before he glanced back at him. His manager's mouth was drawn into a straight line. "Leave her alone, Jesse." The words were quiet. It was advice rather than command, but advice given with the authority of long friendship. "She's not your ordinary camp follower."

"Since when do I take up with ordinary camp followers?"

"She hasn't been around a lot. Dammit, you know that."

"So you're her daddy, now?"

Jack drove for a silent span of highway. "Let's just say I'm a friend...of yours." He kept his eyes straight ahead. "I saw what you did to yourself after Rita died. I don't want to see what you do to yourself if Angel gets hurt out of this."

Jesse didn't answer, but the sudden tension of unspoken words crackled in the air like negatively charged ions.

From the back, Tony leaned forward, then reached across the seat to hand Jesse an unopened pint of Old Turkey. "Ah jes' happened to find this in my pocket," he drawled easily. "You want a belt?"

Jesse glanced back at him, jammed his hat onto his head, then faced forward and crossed his arms over his chest. "I'll wait till we get to Amarillo," he muttered.

At five-thirty Jack's Ford pulled into the lot behind the

theater in Amarillo and parked beside the tour bus, close to
the stage door.

Music was coming over the PA as they walked into the
lobby. The regular sound crew must have already started to
set up, Jesse realized, surprised. He crossed to the half-lit
auditorium, listening. Acoustic guitar, bass and, as he
reached the doorway, the clean, smooth soprano of Angel
Trent.

She was onstage, in profile to the auditorium, facing
Hank, watching the bass player as she sang. Jesse felt
something instinctive, possessive and irrational churn in his
gut.

The ash-blond hair swung as she moved to the beat. She
was playing off a bass line Hank had laid down to an easy,
country-blues tune he'd never heard before. In her voice
there was a sense of improvisation and a shading of emotion that made the words reach out and take him by the
throat, despite the fact that she was singing them to Hank.

> "The distant gleam of city lights
> Was in your eyes today.
> I know you've got to go
> But you know I've got to stay.
> 'Cause in the end your feelings
> Are a thing you can't control.
> You may have my heart
> But this prairie has my soul."

She stepped back from the mike as Carlos moved in on
harmonica. Angel took the lead, matching her bass runs to
Hank's. Hank was grinning ear to ear, and Angel was smiling at him, relaxed and uninhibited. There was something
innocent and unaffected about her pleasure in the music that
was like her: vulnerable, warm, touchable.

"Hot damn," Tony said, next to him. "That sounds real
sweet."

"Sure does," Nancy put in.

Jesse kept his attention turned to the stage. He swallowed down the old, familiar emotion he thought he'd cured himself of in the years with Rita: jealousy. It was tinged, now, with some kind of protective urge, some sense that told him Jack was right. He should leave her alone. He would hurt her. But what he felt in his gut was a primitive, proprietary anger. She should be playing her music with him.

With deliberate effort, he unclenched his fists. "Yeah," he muttered sourly. "Sounds real good."

Nancy was frowning toward the soundboard, manned by one of the theater's regular sound crew. "Why doesn't he turn up the guitar? It needs more treble." She peered toward the stage. "For Pete's sake, what mike is she on? That's a voice mike!"

Tony started walking toward the stage, strolling in time to the music. Nancy went ahead of him, hands thrust purposefully into her pockets, heading for the soundboard.

Jesse stood where he was, watching Angel and his bass player, irritated with himself for finding it so hard to admit they sounded good together. Better than just good. Angel was something special. She had the kind of gift that could take you with her to the rural, close-knit country where the music had started—to a place where the simple human feelings it touched were known with the validity of living them, with neighbors and family that had stayed in one place, together, all their lives. There was an emotion in his throat brought there by the music, but it didn't erase the churning in his stomach.

He pulled his hands out of his pockets and started toward the stage.

The volume on Angel's guitar increased suddenly. She glanced up toward the soundboard, her face registering surprise at Nancy's grin and raised "okay" sign. Then she looked out toward the auditorium, caught sight of Tony and

Jesse, and stepped back from the mike. The music trailed off by instrument: guitar, then harmonica, lastly bass.

"Keep it up, honey," Nancy called to her. "You sound great."

"We were just playing around, waiting for you," she said into the mike. "I'll get out of the way."

"No, no. Keep going," Nancy told her. "Let's get some levels on it."

Angel glanced out at her again. One slim hand came off the guitar to push her hair slowly back on her shoulder. "We were just fooling around, Nancy. We're not going to use it tonight."

There was a beat of surprised silence. "Why not?"

"Sounds real nice," Tony put in from the edge of the stage. "Sounds good just as is."

Angel glanced from Nancy to Tony, then to Jesse, standing beside him at the corner of the stage.

"Look, we were just filling in the time. Just fooling around."

"Well, keep it up," Nancy said again, a note of impatience in her voice. "I'll get the levels set."

She slipped the guitar strap off her shoulders, slowly. "But we're not going to *do* it, Nance...."

"We're not?" Hank asked. "Come on, Angel, it's first-rate stuff. Amarillo will love it."

"Real nice tune," Tony said. "And the bass and the harp are just right with it."

"Yeah, real nice," Frank put in, from the side of the stage.

Angel glanced from one to the other with wariness and a growing trace of apprehension. Hank, questioning, his hands still on the strings of his bass. Nancy, frowning, peering at her over the soundboard. Frank and Tony, curious, interested. Jack, unsmiling and watchful. The easy camaraderie of a few moments ago was suddenly gone, replaced by professional demands that carried the weight of her own unresolved conflicts.

Her wary gaze moved to Jesse. He was standing, silent, his eyes resting on her with the same intensity she'd felt the night before. The heated strength of unspoken demand in his gaze made her throat dry.

One at a time, the members of Jesse's band turned toward him.

Jesse took a couple of steps away from the curtain. "I happen to know the lady won't take requests."

She looked at him, surprised by the unexpected refusal to apply pressure.

Jesse's gaze flicked down over her, the movement quick and almost involuntary, but his eyes lingered briefly on the front pockets of her shirt.

She felt her response as a wave of embarrassed heat in her face. The image of Jesse in her hotel room, his hands on her bare shoulders, his mouth on hers, was impossible to dismiss. Unconsciously she brought her guitar in front of her and looped the strap over her head again.

He didn't have to speak. She knew what he thought of her. An original Prairieland virgin. Someone afraid to compete with her cousin on any level, personal or professional.

Nancy shifted her weight from one foot to the other. Angel glanced up at her. The tanned, self-confident Texas face showed perplexity. Hesitation, Angel knew, was as foreign as a New England winter to the older woman's nature. Her own reluctance must seem like inexplicable, childish timidity.

Angel's mouth wrinkled at the image of herself she could see in five sets of Texas eyes. She swallowed the dryness from her throat and looked out toward Jack, away from Jesse. "All right," she said, the words scratchy.

Jack's burly shoulders hunched as he uncrossed his arms. "You don't have to do it if you don't want to, Angela. It's your decision."

"'Course she wants to," Hank broke in, grinning. "She just said all right. Let's do it!"

There was a collective murmur of approval, punctuated by Nancy's businesslike, "Right."

Hank played a bass run. Angel stepped up close to the microphone, still avoiding Jesse's eyes.

Carlos glanced from Jesse to Angela, then down to his harmonica. He smiled slightly at Angel. "Jess is the real harp player in the band. I bet he'd stand in for you, if you asked him."

She gazed at the harmonica, saying nothing, while seconds stretched out. There was a vaguely uncomfortable silence.

At the edge of the stage, Jesse stood still for a moment, watching her. Then he gave his manager a curt nod, turned on his heel and walked offstage. Most eyes followed him, but not Angel's. Hank's eyebrows rose, and his lips pursed in a silent whistle, but no one spoke.

"Set up the Turner on the guitar, would you, Gil?" Nancy broke in, calling down from the soundboard. "Carlos, you take Frank's mike. Okay, people, from the top. Let's get these levels set."

Jesse crossed the hall in front of the stage and sat down beside Jack.

Angel put her hands where they belonged on her guitar, and took it from the top.

Four hours later, under the colored lights of the stage, in front of a packed house, she used the arrangement as an encore to her set. It brought the most enthusiastic ovation she'd had since they'd started the tour. When she'd finished the song, she stood on the stage, pleased and a little disconcerted as she listened to the applause and the calls for *more*! with real surprise.

Hank leaned toward her. "Want to do another one?" he asked.

She glanced at him, made a quick decision and shook her head, then stepped back to the microphone, smiling. "Thank you," she said when the applause had quieted to satisfied murmuring. "But I expect we're all ready for Jesse Adam Wilson."

It had been the right thing to say. There was more applause, eager and expectant, for the star they had come to see. As if it had been planned, Jesse appeared from the wings to take her place at the microphone.

He must have been waiting there, watching her, she realized, in case he was needed for just such a scenario as this. Looped over his shoulders was the electric guitar he usually played at the end of his set for fast-paced, rock-country songs. Serita's eagle feathers were not on the neck.

He didn't want to compete in any way with her performance. The sudden thought surprised her into glancing at him as they passed on the stage. He nodded, tipped his hat, then gave her a quick grin and a thumbs-up sign.

The small, unexpected chivalry made her feel a twinge of guilt for refusing to perform with him. He could have taken the refusal personally. But he hadn't.

"Miss Angel Trent," he was saying into the PA system when she turned to watch him from behind the curtain. "A lady we're all gonna hear more from in the future."

He led another round of applause for her before he launched into a rock tune, with Hank on bass, that gave the rest of his band a chance to come onstage and join in as the spirit moved them. It was smooth, professional and impressive. It was done with a style that was his hallmark. His instincts were perfectly on target, as usual.

And he'd been right about her music.

She gazed out at the stage for another long moment, watching Jesse, the neck of his guitar conspicuously unadorned. She hadn't expected that sensitivity from him—to start out with an electric guitar so that there would be no comparison to her—and to have put aside, tonight, the talisman of her cousin and predecessor.

And yet, she should have expected it. That kind of unadvertised sensitivity was an essential part of Jesse's character. Why did it always come as a surprise to her? She felt a twinge of remorse. She always expected the worst from him because everything else about him was a threat: his blunt honesty, his talent, the sexuality that electrified his performances and that he wore like a tailored cowboy shirt wherever he appeared.

Her heart beat faster at the thought of Jesse in her hotel room. He'd been bluntly honest about what he wanted from her then, too.

She was the one who hadn't been able to say what she wanted. She couldn't explain the potent fear that was—just barely—stronger than the fierce physical hunger he could call up from her at will.

Yeah, you have a real good idea of who you're not.

Her hand moved from her billowy, white lawn skirt to the bodice of her camisole. The delicate, ribbon-edged stage garment was laced up the front with silk cord, but Angel's hand, unconsciously, was holding up an unbuttoned silk dress.

You're afraid you can't fill Serita's moccasins. Is that it?

The intrusive image of Serita, haunting and destructive as a childhood superstition, rose in her mind.

Onstage, Jesse's song ended and he moved into a familiar love ballad, one he usually performed with his acoustic guitar. He had no trouble transposing it to the electric instrument he was playing. He could have played it, she thought wryly, on a comb with waxed paper and made it work. He put his feelings out onstage, unpolished, unedited, real. That stage persona was the flip side to a complex and contradictory personality. There was a current of feeling under the hard cynicism that surfaced in surprising ways.

I did what I could to help her, Angel...

The echo of his words rippled through her consciousness like a ghost—like Serita's spirit, unable to rest because it had sold its soul for this life....

Angel turned abruptly, put her guitar back in its case, and walked out through the wings. An exit corridor ran along the side of the auditorium to the front of the building. She followed it to the deserted lobby, then let herself into the back of the darkened concert hall. The door swung shut behind her, silently, and the darkness gradually lifted as her eyes adjusted to it. There was an empty seat near the side aisle a few rows in front of her. She made her way to it and sat down.

The dim theater had the vaguely definable smell of an auditorium—tobacco, soda, perfume, beer—and the comforting anonymity of crowded darkness. All eyes were on the stage. Even from the back of the auditorium she could feel the power of Jesse's performance. He put his soul into it.

Beside her, a teenage girl leaned forward in rapt adoration and let out a worshipful sigh as Jesse ended the verse to the love ballad. Angel shot her a covert glance. It was easy to identify with the girl. Jesse's music had an emotional appeal Angel had felt since she'd been that age herself. In a strange way the distant, lighted figure on the stage seemed more real, more accessible, than the flesh-and-blood man who had touched her the night before.

A swift, electrifying thrill of unnameable panic ran through her, all the more heart stopping because it followed no clear line of reason. She only knew it was connected somehow to Jesse, to the thought of herself up on that stage, to the image of herself in a motel room with Jesse—giving away her soul.

She must have made some sound. The girl beside her turned to give her a brief, lovelorn, I-know-what-you-mean smile, then went back to her rapt listening.

Angel settled farther into her seat, and leaned her head back against the edge of it.

She sat through the rest of the concert and two encores, then stayed in her seat, unmoving, her head bent into her palm, elbow on the armrest, while the houselights came up and the concertgoers laughed and chattered their way toward the exits.

In fits and surges, the crowd thinned out. Several people gave her curious glances as they walked by her seat, but most were intent on conversation or the business of leaving the hall. No one recognized her. She wasn't Jesse Wilson.

She wasn't Serita.

When the theater was almost empty, she got up and walked down the aisle.

Onstage, Gil was packing up the last monitor, winding a cord around his arm. The wings were in semidarkness. All the equipment and instruments had been taken out, but her guitar case lay where she'd left it. The crew knew enough not to move it unless she asked them to.

She crossed to the case and crouched in front of it, checked her guitar, then snapped the locks.

"Where were you?"

She didn't have to turn her head to know that the softly spoken question was Jesse's. The low voice stirred her senses like a fingertip along her spine. She stood up slowly, hesitating a moment before she swung around to face him.

"I was out in the auditorium." Her voice, to her surprise, was level, but nervous tension was humming along her veins, frightening, exhilarating and dangerous. "I sat through your performance."

"What'd it sound like?"

"It sounded . . . like Jesse Adam Wilson. There isn't anyone to compare to it. Nobody else can do a performance like you."

In the dim light she couldn't read his expression.

"I wasn't out in the auditorium watching you, Angel, but it sounded real good from back here."

"Thanks."

"Sounded good this afternoon, too, when I walked in. It was—real good when you were playing up here with Hank and Carlos."

The unpretending honesty in the rough voice made her feel small and indefensibly guilty. She smiled uncertainly and looked away. "We were just fooling around with some songs on the bus, and then, waiting for you, we just kept on with it."

"It was worth keeping on with."

She dropped her gaze again, uncomfortable in his presence, too aware of the empty theater, the late-night intimacy. "Has everyone gone?"

"Yeah. You sat out there quite a while."

"I know." One hand fidgeted with the narrow shoulder strap of her camisole. "I can't get used to playing in a place this size. For an audience that comes to hear people like you and Serita. I was just thinking."

"About what?"

She shrugged.

"Being able to sit in a hall without causing a small riot?"

She gave a huff of laughter. "Something like that, I suppose."

In the darkness, with the black hat and dark hair, and shadowed, almost-black eyes, the dangerous appeal of his grin sent a shiver down her spine. Awareness tingled at the back of her neck. "Listen, Jesse. I know you did whatever you could to make it work for me tonight—with the electric guitar, not having the eagle feathers—" Her hand slid around to the nape of her neck. "Thanks, for that."

"You didn't need much help, singing the way you do, writing songs like that."

She met his gaze.

"It's a great tune," he said. "Made me want to move to Nebraska to see if I could take the place of whatever man who'd be fool enough to walk out on you."

Her hand moved around to the front of her throat.

Jesse watched her, his expression serious, unsmiling. "No one was thinking about Rita when you were singing it."

Her throat worked as she swallowed again. Her nervous fingers traced the edge of her camisole.

Jesse's glance followed the slight movement. Behind him, one of the stage lights flicked off. The remaining backlighting diminished in steps as the houselights went out.

"I suppose we'd better be going," Angel said. "We'll be leaving Texas in the morning, right?"

"Yeah. To Kansas. Then South Dakota."

She nodded.

"There's something else I didn't get around to telling you this afternoon," he said. "Serita's benefit concert has been rescheduled, provided there's no trouble between now and then."

"Oh." The word came out on a shocked breath. She felt a sudden knot of tension in her stomach, and covered it with a quick, forced smile. "Well that's great, Jesse."

He nodded, his serious gaze still on her face, the dark eyes studying her with unwavering purpose.

"That's what you want, isn't it?"

He didn't answer for a moment, then his eyes moved down to the lacing holding the white lawn camisole together at the bodice. He took a slow step toward her, then reached out to pick up the end of a silk lacing. When he spoke, the rough voice was intimate and low. "What I want is to untie this ribbon. Then I want to pull it out all the way down. I want to take a long time finding out if you're wear ing that lacy thing under it. I want to take my time with that little piece of lace...."

Abruptly she turned away and bent down to her guitar case. The picture shimmered in front of her, alive with detail her own mind was all too willing to supply.

She squared her shoulders and stood up, picking up the guitar case by the handle.

Jesse didn't move, but one corner of his mouth curved up. He looked sexy and disquietingly intriguing. "You don't want me to do that, Angel?"

A wave of heat shimmered through her body. She wasn't wearing a bra under the lined camisole, and against the smooth material her breasts ached for his touch. Her voice, caught in her throat, was husky. "That's not a fair question."

"No," he said, against her expectations. "I suppose not."

That oddly unexpected capitulation tugged at her emotions as strongly as the sexual urges and the warning panic. "Jesse—" she took a small step toward him, made a small gesture with her free hand, palm up.

His gaze, following her gesture, darkened perceptibly in the dim light. When he looked up at her face there was a sudden blaze of uncloaked passion in his eyes that brought an electric chill singing along her nerves. She dropped her hand to her side, her eyes wide and wary.

A flicker of sharp disappointment came and went in his face, fleeting, elusive, and replaced almost instantaneously by a cynical curve to his mouth. "You're right. You'd just get hurt."

She didn't answer him, but she frowned in troubled puzzlement. She'd seen that flash of disillusionment in his face. It put a claim on her emotions that wouldn't bear questioning, but that couldn't, for all her wariness, be dismissed.

"There's a cab out front, waiting for you," Jesse said flatly. "He'll take you back to the hotel."

"You're ... going out?"

"Yeah," he said harshly. "I'm going out." He gave her another glance, then took a step toward her and held a hand out for her guitar case. She swung it toward him. His fingers touched hers on the handle of the case when he took it from her, and the touch lingered there for a fraction of a second before he moved away from her and turned toward the stage door. "Come on."

Her hands felt empty. Her whole body felt empty. The thought of letting him walk away into that private, disillusioned, cynical world was ... desolating.

I did what I could for her, Angel.

And he had blamed himself, ever since.

"What if I don't want to go back to the hotel?" she said suddenly, impulsively.

He looked back at her cynically. "Where do you think you want to go?"

"It's my last night in Texas. Maybe I want to see Amarillo." He watched her, silent. "I just played one of my own songs for the biggest crowd that's ever heard it," she went on. "Maybe I want to go out for a beer."

"You're making a mistake, Angel."

"By going out for a beer?"

"With me?"

She shrugged, crossing her arms in front of her, hugging her elbows, elaborately casual. "I just thought you might know of a place."

He stared at her for a moment, then his gaze flicked down over her, swiftly, and moved away to the curtains. He glanced back at her and his mouth curved in a wry smile. "I know all of 'em," he told her. "Where do you want to start?"

Six

———

A warm Amarillo wind fluttered Angel's skirt around her legs as she and Jesse walked toward the waiting cab in front of the auditorium. Neither of them spoke. Jesse's boots made a measured rhythm on the pavement, heavier than her low-heeled slippers, his steps longer than hers. Her heart was racing as fast as her unbiddable thoughts. He carried the guitar between them, as if it were needed as a barrier. Angel put her hands in her pockets and pressed her palms against her thighs, trying not to think of the implications of what she was doing.

The air smelled of Texas: cattle, earth and the half-civilized but unmistakable aura of Texas lawlessness. In the warm, dry wind, she shivered.

Jesse turned toward her and his footsteps halted.

"Cold?" His gaze dropped to her bare arms and shoulders.

She shook her head. "No, not really."

He ignored her answer, shrugging his denim jacket off his shoulders. He set her guitar case down and held the jacket out for her.

"I'm not . . ." Her protest trailed off. She turned, with a tense smile, to let him help her with the jacket.

His hands brushed along her shoulders in a brief caress that sent shivers of panic down her spine even after he dropped his hands, abruptly, and picked up the guitar. He waited for her to walk on, and she complied, wearing his jacket, her legs unsteady beneath her.

The cabbie waiting at the curb was reading a magazine. He flipped it closed and stuffed it under the seat as Angel climbed into the cab. Self-conscious, she pulled the denim jacket closed at the front.

"Ma'am." The cabbie gave her a boyish, gap-toothed grin, tipped his hat, and smiled at Jesse as he got in beside her. "Where'll it be, Jesse? Back to your *ho*-tel? Y'all don't mind if ah call ya Jesse, do ya?"

"Nope." Jesse's gaze flicked to Angel, and stayed there. "Across town. The Belle Texas," he said, looking at her.

"Sure thang, pardner."

The guitar was propped between them, Jesse's elbow on top of it. The cabbie eyed the arrangement in the rearview mirror with unconcealed curiosity that settled, in leisurely assessment, on Angela.

"You're Angel Trent, aren't ya?"

"Yes."

In the mirror, the cabbie's eyebrows rose and he grinned at Jesse, man-to-man.

Jesse shot Angel a look of worldly amusement, but underneath it he was studying her face, assessingly, taking heed of her reaction.

In spite of herself, she felt revealing color rise in her cheeks.

The cabbie grinned again, delighted. He turned his eyes back to the road and started whistling. The song was Jesse's current single: *Make Me Love You Tonight*. He followed it by the flip side. The lyrics repeated themselves in Angel's mind: *I don't want to lie to you, Baby...I don't want to lie here alone....*

She turned toward the window, willing her emotions to slow down, her stomach to unknot. She was going out for a beer after a concert, with another musician. There was nothing in this situation to fuel the imaginings of a curious cabdriver. But it was Jesse Adam Wilson who sat with her in this cab, on the other side of her guitar, and it was her own fantasies that were bringing the heat to her face.

The image of Jesse onstage, multicolored lights glinting on his dark-clad figure, the rough voice edged with intimate emotion, smoldered in her imagination.

Three tunes later they pulled into the parking lot of a wooden-shingled, rambling, one-story building set down on a strip of white stucco hotels and restaurants on the west side of Amarillo. Over the red saloon-style doors the words Belle Texas flashed in neon. The sounds of a country-music band blared out of the bar as some of the crowd spilled outside, raucous, genial, the men holding beers, the women laughing and flirting with them.

It was the kind of place Serita might have favored. Angel slid out of the cab and stood looking around her, awkward and ill at ease, while Jesse paid the cabdriver and got out with her guitar. He took her elbow, glanced down at her carefully schooled expression, then gave her an ironic, proprietary grin. "The Belle's the best place in Amarillo to hear music," he said. "It's been here for years."

"I can imagine."

"Y'all have a good time, now!" the cabdriver yelled out the window. "Next time you're in town, I'm gonna catch your concert, Jesse. And yours, too, Angel!" He pulled out, crossed against the traffic, and gave them a grin and a wave from the street, playing to the small stir he'd made with his announcement.

Interested heads turned toward them, and the raucous conversation around the door quieted. Jesse steered her past the onlookers with a polite, casual, "Evening," to the crowd in general, keeping his hand on her elbow. Angel managed a smile, nervously uncomfortable, her awareness focused on Jesse's possessive touch through the denim sleeve of his jacket.

The interior of the Belle was dim, smoky and crowded. Directly to the left of the entrance was a long bar. The bartender was doing a brisk trade. A blue-jeaned cowboy at one end caught Angela's eye as she and Jesse walked in. He turned, elbows resting on the rounded edge of the bar, and looked her over, adjusting his hat. Jesse gave him a level stare, then nodded to him once, and put his hand on the middle of her back, guiding her past the would-be rival. The cowboy turned away. She walked beside Jesse, acutely aware of the male ritual that proclaimed her off limits. The touch of Jesse's fingers branded her through the worn denim of his jacket.

Music was coming from a stage at the back of the large room. On the parqueted dance floor in front of the stage, couples with their arms around each other danced Texas-style to the sounds of a pedal-steel guitar backed up by bass, rhythm and fiddle. The band was good, and the bar's patrons, between the business of drinking, dancing and checking each other out, were giving it enthusiastic attention. Jesse got halfway across the room before he was recognized. In the buzz of suddenly subdued conversation, she heard her own name mentioned. Surprised, she glanced up into the eyes of a big, blond cattleman.

"Evening," Jesse said to him, unsmiling. He nodded back and touched his fingers to his hat brim.

Jesse steered her toward one of the small tables clustered around the dance floor, keeping his hand on her back. He slid the guitar under a table, then pulled out Angela's chair before he sat down across from her. On the spot where his hand had been, tingles of awareness replaced the pressure of his fingers.

The bar was raucous, genial, its ambience somewhere between the Grange hall where her parents enjoyed their Saturday nights out and the smoky, beer-filled pool parlor she and her friends had been forbidden to enter. In Texas, the two seemed to coexist amicably. In her own eyes she seemed foreign. She was a Nebraska folksinger in a Texas honky-tonk, and she felt as naive and unschooled as the teenage girl beside her in the theater who had sighed over Jesse's love song.

A waitress in cowboy hat, painted-on jeans and shirt un-snapped to accentuate her ample cleavage trotted toward the table and greeted them. ''Y'all are Jesse Adam Wilson, ain't ya, honey?''

Jesse tipped his hat to her.

''The boys said y'all come in and sat in my station.''

''I guess the boys were right.''

''Well, hot damn! What can I bring ya?'' Her full-voltage smile beamed like a spotlight. More heads turned nearby and conversations lapsed while the neighboring customers craned their necks for a look at Jesse.

''A couple of Lone Stars,'' Jesse said.

''Comin' right up.'' She smiled and winked. ''Honey.''

Jesse watched her go, then turned back to Angel. He searched her face for a moment, serious, then his mouth quirked wryly and he leaned toward her. ''You wanted to see Texas, Angel.''

''I wanted to see Texas.'' She made herself smile back. ''I guess I wasn't ready for how much Texas wanted to see you.''

His smile faded as he continued to study her face. ''I might say the same,'' he told her.

She looked down at the table. When she looked up again, Jesse's gaze was still on her face, his eyes dark, steady, purposeful.

"You're really at home here, aren't you?" she asked him. "It doesn't bother you to be recognized. To have everyone notice you."

He shrugged. "Sometimes it does. When I think about it."

"But not now?"

"Not now." His gaze rested on her face for a moment, then swept down past her shoulders, to where the denim jacket hung open to her waist, revealing a swathe of ivory skin, satin ribbon and white cotton beneath which her heart fluttered in response to that gaze.

She felt a flush rise in her face, a wave of heat in her body inside the jacket. The temperature in the room was too warm for denim, she realized, but it hadn't occurred to her to take the jacket off. Not when she was sitting across from Jesse and thinking about how much she wanted him.

Her breath caught in her throat. The eyes of the interested bargoers suddenly seemed distant, her awareness of them overwhelmed by the compelling, charismatic gaze of Jesse Adam Wilson, intense, male, real and disturbingly personal.

She shouldn't be here with him. He had warned her himself of what would happen if she came with him.

They both knew what was going to happen.

She felt conscious of the thin material of the camisole against her breasts, of the edging of satin ribbon that tied at the center of the low neckline.

She had known it when she asked him out for a beer. It had been ordained from the moment they'd stepped out of the theater. And it had been more than half her doing that she was here.

Carefully casual, she shrugged out of the jacket. She wasn't quite able to meet Jesse's gaze as she did it.

He sat perfectly still, but she could feel him looking at her, his gaze drifting over her bare arms and shoulders, the lacings between her breasts. In the warm room, another shiver traveled down her spine.

The waitress approached the table, set two bottles of beer in front of them, and grinned. Her eyes took in Angel's low-necklined camisole with swift feminine appraisal, then moved back to Jesse. "It's on the house, honey. You just holler if you want more."

"Thanks."

The woman grinned at Angel. "You better take good care of him, honey. Or I will." She winked again, then trotted off.

Angel kept her eyes fixed on the beer in front of her.

The amenities of the house didn't include glasses. She raised the bottle, and awkwardly sipped from it. Putting it back on the table she traced the wet ring where it had initially sat, all the while avoiding Jesse's eyes.

"Would you like a glass? They've probably got one back there somewhere."

She managed a smile. "Wouldn't I be conspicuous if I got up to ask for a glass?"

Jesse nodded, slowly. His eyes flicked down over her torso. "Yeah."

The music had changed to a slow ballad in three-quarter time. In front of them on the dance floor, a couple drifted by, their arms locked around each other, the young man's cheek resting on his partner's temple, his hands moving on her back, their steps synchronized and slow. The girl turned her head and pressed more closely against her partner, her body joined to his from shoulder to knee.

Angel looked away from them, her thoughts misted with growing passion.

"Would you like to dance?"

Her throat closed. The panic she felt was immediate and tactile. "I don't usually dance. I'm always performing."

He stood, took a step around the table, and held out his hand to her. "Come on."

It was the same gesture she had made to him, in the wings of the darkened theater, when he had warned her against him. Her heart started to pound.

She took his hand, stood up, and let him lead her out to the dance floor.

He kept her hand wrapped in his strong fingers, but turned her toward him and put his arm around her back. The live music surrounded them, loud, close, slow. The slide guitar and the fiddle were leading the melody of a waltz. She could feel the vibrations of the low notes in the floor under their feet.

Jesse held her six inches away from him, as if, she thought, the guitar were still between them. His hand on her back was barely touching her, but his fingers sent out tiny bolts of sensation that made her breath catch in her throat.

Under her palm, resting on his shoulder, she could feel the heat of his body through the material of his black shirt. He smelled of starched cotton and lime.

He moved almost as stiffly as she did. He was careful not to touch her, but his gaze stayed unwaveringly on her face.

A thrill of terror, eroticism and anticipation shot through her. She stumbled over her own feet and fell against Jesse. Her breasts, in the thin camisole, pressed against his hard chest as her hand clutched his shoulder.

"I'm sorry." She pushed herself away from him, but his arm tightened suddenly around her back, holding her body against his as he brushed her hair with the side of his face and pulled her hand, suddenly onto his chest.

A rush of panic laced with hot, sweet desire gripped her. She made a small sound deep in her throat. Jesse's arm tightened around her in response.

"Let's gō," he said with rough urgency.

He turned her, his arm circling her shoulders, and walked her back toward their table. With one movement he snatched up his denim jacket and reached under the table for her guitar. He straightened and guided her back through the crowded bar, her side tucked against him, his arm wrapped possessively around her.

The air outside was cool after the heated closeness of the bar. The sounds of the street seemed subdued after the noise of the Belle. Wind lifted her hair, then made it flutter back on her bare shoulders.

This time no one recognized Jesse. The people outside the door were too busy with their Saturday night joshing, bursts of shared laughter and uninterrupted conversation to notice as Jesse walked Angela across the sidewalk. They paused at the curb. An empty cab was parked a few spaces down the street. Jesse raised his hand from Angela's shoulder to beckon it, and the driver pulled up and stopped in front of them.

"Where to, sir?" the driver asked mechanically.

"The Seguarro," Jesse said.

It was not the hotel where the band was booked to stay. They would have, for tonight anyway, the luxury of separation from the tour group who knew each other's everyday lives in unavoidable detail. The privacy was something she needed, she realized, yet it wouldn't have occurred to her to take it in this way. She glanced at Jesse, but he didn't comment.

The guitar, this time was not between them. Jesse's hand reached toward her to touch a lock of hair. He folded it between fingers and thumb, exploring the texture, letting it slide over his knuckle.

The short cab ride passed in silence, but his gaze was dark, heated with intent.

The Seguarro was a four-story, white stucco structure that looked much like the string of hotels neighboring it.

Jesse paid the cabbie, who showed no interest in them except as fares. Cloaked in anonymity, he and Angela walked into the lobby and crossed an expanse of rust-colored carpeting to a long wooden desk flanked by potted cactus.

There was a lounge opposite the desk, where western-clothed Amarillo businessmen drank sedately. She felt conspicuous and out of her element, wryly aware that her own thoughts were probably racier than any in the minds of the hotel clientele.

Jesse dropped his arm from her shoulder, put both palms flat on the desk and said, "We'd like a room."

The desk clerk smiled, bored. He consulted the register. "Certainly, sir. We have a double on the fourth floor." He glanced up at Jesse, then gave Angel a quick, discreet once-over and looked back at the register.

"Fine," Jesse said.

"Will that be cash or ch—" He cut himself off as Jesse pulled his wallet from his back pocket. At the bar in the lounge, one of the men glanced toward them casually. In spite of herself, Angel felt a wave of heat creep up her neck. Embarrassed she stared at her feet, convinced her imaginings must show in her face.

The clerk rang up Jesse's money, handed him a key and slid the register toward him.

"Fourth floor, to the right of the elevators, Mr..." There was a diplomatic pause as he glanced at the illegible register and substituted, "Sir."

Jesse had already turned toward her, touched the small of her back, and started toward the bank of elevators.

She felt the desk clerk's eyes on them all the way across the lobby.

Jesse's hand moved up to the nape of her neck, massaging the tight, corded muscles that revealed her tension. He tipped his head toward her. "This is Texas, Angel. People do this all the time," he said into her ear.

She laughed, embarrassed, not looking at him.

Waiting for the elevator, he stood without touching her. She skimmed a swift, sidelong glance at him, then asked him a question she needed answered. "Do you . . . do this all the time?"

He waited for her to look back at him. "Only in my mind," he said. His voice had a texture of burred honesty as he added, "Since the day you walked into that audition, I've done this a hundred times. Always with you."

Something fluttered in her stomach.

"There hasn't been a night I haven't had you in my bed, Angel." His voice was a soft growl. "You know that."

The realization that she, too, had shared this impending intimacy with Jesse startled her. He stirred some fantasy in her mind that she could neither dismiss nor subdue.

The elevator doors slid open and Jesse touched her shoulder again as she walked in. She stood, her gaze fixed on the lighted numbers of the panel as the elevator carried them up to their floor. When her glance slipped toward Jesse he was watching her steadily.

Their room was two doors from the elevator. Jesse fit the key into the lock and swung the door open.

The decor suited a Texas cattleman's taste. Western-theme paintings and a collection of ten-gallon hats hung on the walls. Brightly colored Mexican rugs covered the pine floor. Next to a brass bed was a nightstand with spatterware pitcher and bowl.

Jesse set her guitar down and turned toward her, his mouth quirked. "You wanted Texas, Angel." The words were light, but there was a husky catch in his voice that didn't match his flippancy. What she had wanted—what she had agreed to—made her throat dry. Her heart thudded out an agitated rhythm beneath her cotton camisole.

"I...wanted Texas," she admitted, her voice as husky as his, but as if in denial of the words, she folded her arms in front of her, hugging her upper arms, the message of her body language anxious and unsure.

Jesse closed the distance between them with two slow, deliberate steps. He gazed down at her. "I couldn't wait any longer for this, Angel," he said.

There was a charged silence while she, too, waited what seemed like an eternity for her voice to give an answer she couldn't quite utter.

With agonizing slowness he reached up to trace the edge of her jaw with the callused tip of one finger. The back of his knuckle stroked down the side of her neck, where the tension inside her was betrayed by taut muscles. "Don't ask me to, Angel." The gruff murmur was both a demand and a plea, and it reached out to touch her emotions as surely as his fingers were touching her flesh.

Her breath escaped in a long, trembling sigh. Her eyelids fluttered closed, and she raised her hand to his, feathering her fingers over the back of his knuckles.

Jesse's strong fingers opened. His palm slid around her neck and his mouth came down onto hers.

His lips caressed and coaxed, moving on hers with gentle pressure, while both his hands threaded into her hair to tip her head back farther. The anxious tremors of her heart calmed, beguiled at the touch of his hands and his mouth, and she let her own arms encircle his wide back, hardly aware of her actions.

She felt the tip of his tongue between her lips and opened her mouth to him. Jesse took what she offered and more, exploring her opened mouth with consummate, devastating skill, he stroked and caressed with liquid, sensate plundering that sedated her resistance and chased her doubts like so much dust before a Texas wind.

He slid one hand down her spine to the middle of her back, urging her against him. She yielded to the touch, letting him gather her close against the hard muscles of his chest. Her every heartbeat seemed to send a pulse of sensation racing along her veins.

Ecstatic ripples of pleasure fanned out to erase the anxious panic of moments before. Warm wantonness shimmered through her, and she surrendered to it unequivocally. She answered Jesse's kiss with a mounting passion of her own that she had no thought of controlling, returning his hunger with a wild, eager physical hunger of her own.

The gentle pressure of his kiss suddenly became demanding, the enticing caress became an invasion, primal and possessive. Jesse's widespread palms pressed against her shoulder blades, the small of her back, her hips, her buttocks, molding her body against the length of his, letting her feel the strength of his arms, the tension in the muscles of his torso, his hard arousal. Pliant and willing, she pressed against him. Hot, sweet desire flared through her, catalyzed by a seed of panic that had become ardent need.

Jesse broke off the kiss. His hands retraced their path up her back to thread into her hair. His breath was a harsh rasp, and at his throat she could see his pulse beating as rapidly as hers.

"Lord, Angel, I've been thinkin' about this since the first time I saw you...."

His eyes searched her face. His gaze was intense, impassioned, as if he sought contact with her soul.

She felt her heart stop for an instant, and her lips opened as she gazed back at him.

Jesse's palms slid down the sides of her neck. One hand moved to the front of her throat, then traced her collarbone and the edge of her camisole. "Everything you've ever had on I've taken off you in my mind about five different ways, wondering when you'd let me do it."

Her hands fell still, encircling his rib cage. Her voice was breathless. She smiled tremulously as she confessed, "I've let you do it in my mind long since...."

He took the silk cord between his fingers, twisting it around thumb and forefinger, watching her face, inch by inch, he pulled out the bow and hooked his finger in the first silk cross to work it loose.

The tug of his fingers on the laces pulled her camisole lightly against her breasts, sending faint, erotic, enervating currents fanning out from the peaks of her breasts to her stomach, her thighs, her knees. He hesitated a moment, his fingers brushing the valley between her breasts, then he pulled the second cross loose.

A flood of sensation was released within her as she let him undress her, pulling out the cords down to the waist of her camisole, where it was held together by a tiny hook. He left the hook fastened and pushed open the front of the camisole, his fingers exploring the ribbon-edged garment, almost, but not quite, tracing the contours of her body.

Her breasts ached for his touch, the nipples rigid, pointed, sensitive, it seemed, to his gaze, his heartbeat, his very imaginings.

A breath of need escaped from her throat, expressive and evocative as music. In answer to it, Jesse cupped her breasts with his palms, caressing and kneading. Her fists closed around handfuls of his shirt, unconsciously twisting as he touched and stroked, building the fires within her.

"Angel..." His rough, low voice was shaded with desire. "Angel... you felt good, in my mind, but never this good...."

Her hands tugged at his shirt, pulling it out of his jeans, then went sliding up under it. She sought the texture of skin and muscle, needing to touch him.

Jesse bent his head to the hollow of her shoulder to blaze a hot, damp path up the side of her neck and around to the front of her throat. His lips left a trail of delight in the wake of his mouth, while his hands still shaped and reshaped soft breast and hardened nipple.

Without warning, he pulled away from her. Her skirt was swept into the back of her knees as he lifted her, and carried her across the room.

Bedsprings creaked under their combined weight as he sat on the edge of the mattress, then twisted to lay her down on the cotton blanket, leaning over her, cupping her passion-flushed face in his hands. His mouth covered hers again, briefly, but he broke the kiss off to trace a sensuous trail down her neck, between her collarbones, at the hollow of her breasts.

His mouth circumscribed the outer edge of one soft, resilient mound before he wet its crest with his mouth, teasing and tormenting with lips and tongue, moving to the other breast to coax the budding nipple into a sweet agony of arousal.

Angel ran her fingers into his hair, then under the collar of his shirt and around to the front of it. She pulled open the top snap and tugged at the material now trapped between their bodies.

"What do you want, Angel?" Jesse murmured, his voice a ragged thread of breath against the sensitized peak of her breast. "Tell me. Say it."

"I want you...to make love to me. I want you with me..."

His mouth still at her breast, he fumbled at the snaps of his shirt. He shrugged it off and let it lie where it fell, rustling, on the floor. The exquisite torment of his tongue and teeth left her as he sat up to unsnap and unzip his jeans.

Her breasts were full and aching, the tips wet from his mouth, acutely sensitive to the cool air of the room. She crossed her arms over them, shivering, watching Jesse.

He fumbled in his pocket and pulled out a small, foil-wrapped package. "Do I need this?" he asked, his voice gruff, tender, low pitched.

She nodded.

Without speaking, he pulled off his boots, stood, and stripped off his jeans, then leaned over her. His long, lean body was hard with controlled tension, the muscles of his chest and torso rigidly defined. Slowly, gently, he took her wrists to uncross her arms and pin her wrists to the pillow.

He let go of her hands as he kissed her, and she clung to him, tracing the muscles of his shoulders, back and hips with eager hands, while Jesse unfastened her skirt and pulled it down from her waist. She raised her hips to let him slide it under her. The soft material whispered as it tumbled to the floor beside Jesse's jeans.

She wanted him immediately. When he touched her she let out a gasped, broken moan of desire.

"Angel..." Jesse said again. The single word was a ragged sound of need, physical, emotional, spiritual. As if in some unexpected way he wanted to erase his long, self-imposed emptiness.

She wrapped her hands around his buttocks and guided him into her, and then their bodies were moving, beat for beat, need for need. Together they left thought, reason, words behind, like a single note drawn out to unbearable, heart-rending beauty, higher...higher...until the tension broke into a shattering, chorused release. Angela clutched at Jesse's shoulders and uttered a single cry and his sound of climax followed hers as he called out her name in a litany of need and possession.

Slowly, to the sound of her name on Jesse's lips, she drifted down from the maelstrom of that wild rush of passion. She was trembling and Jesse held her close to him, his palm widespread on her back, a hand tucking her head into the hollow of his shoulder as he gathered her against his body. He held her close, murmuring her name softly. Gradually she felt his heartbeat slow and his strong arm loosened around her.

Under her cheek, his chest was damp. Angel let her eyes drift closed, breathing in the scent of soap, sweat, a faint suggestion of starched cotton on his skin. She ran her fingers lightly along the ridge of muscle on his chest, then pulled away from him slightly to look up at his face. His arm tightened around her back in subconscious reaction before he relaxed it to let her go. His chest rose and fell, then his hand moved to her hair. His fingers, combing through the tangled coils, were shaky.

Slowly he grinned and his chest lifted in a brief, unbelieving chuckle. "I was going to take my time with that, Angel. I was going to make it so good for you you wouldn't be able to say no."

She ran her fingers across his chest again. "I don't recall saying no."

He smiled again, wryly. "I don't recall givin' you much of a chance."

He studied her face. His fingers brushed her hair away from it, then his smile faded and his expression grew serious with some dark, self-searching honesty. "I don't think I would've stopped even if you had, Angel. I don't think anything in heaven or hell would have stopped me."

Her hand ceased its leisurely exploration. Beneath the cynical warning she sensed a current of self-recrimination and disillusionment that didn't usually surface. She didn't understand, but her reaction was instinctive, feminine, unneedful of understanding.

She laid her palm against his cheek, propping herself up on one elbow to lean over him. Slowly she brought her mouth down onto his, her lips open to caress and seduce in an ancient, timeless communication.

Jesse lay beneath her, complying when she pressed a hand against his shoulder to make him roll onto his back. His hand threaded through her hair, then moved along her shoulder in a slow, caressing curve. His mouth moved against hers, responsive and skilled, in unhurried give-and-take of explorative, elemental sensuality.

"Angel..." he said once, murmuring the word into her mouth.

There was no question of time or pace, measure or meaning in the slow sharing that followed, as in the small hours of the night Jesse let her into the dark reaches of his soul.

Seven

The soft, mellow notes of a guitar drifted into Angela's consciousness before she was fully awake. Someone was playing music.

She could feel the heat of sunshine on her arm and shoulder, soft and warm as the unexamined feeling of well-being that trickled through her half-awake thoughts.

She opened her eyes. Jesse.

Sunlight slanted across his bare chest and touched the side of his face. He was sitting at the foot of the bed, wearing only his jeans, his back against the wall, his legs stretched out across the bedspread, her guitar in his lap.

He glanced across at her and smiled.

Still sleepy, she smiled back. Under the bed covers, she sat up and wrapped her arms around her bent knees. Warm sun fell on her exposed back. They'd forgotten to close the drapes.

She made a soft sound and pulled a hand out from under the sheet to rub the sleep out of her eyes. "Why didn't you wake me up?" she murmured.

"I was watching you sleep. You looked so innocent. Like an angel."

She gave a small chuckle.

The light brought out dark glints in his hair. She'd seldom seen him without his hat. His hair was thick, almost raven-black, unruly. She had the urge to run her fingers through it, to tame it. Instead, she brushed a strand of her own hair out of her face.

He leaned toward her, supporting his weight on one hand, then reached for her and kissed her over the rim of the guitar. His mouth was light, gentle, expert. Remembered sensations wafted through her, and along with them the memory of her own passion. He had made her forget everything but him.

He could do so again. They both knew it.

He sat back against the wall, watching her, satisfied, his body and shoulders relaxed.

A shiver, like the breath of an unexpected presence, flicked down her spine.

Outside the window, the noise of a truck at a loading dock drifted up from the street, where the day's business was being conducted. Angel's glance flicked toward the brightly lit window. The sun was high; it must be midmorning.

Her watch was facedown on the night table. She reached for it and turned it over in her hand.

"What time is it?" Jesse asked.

"Ten-fifteen." She looked up at him, wide-eyed and chagrined. "We're supposed to be leaving at ten-thirty, aren't we?"

He shrugged, but made no move to get up. His fingers played on the strings of the guitar.

Her mouth quirked with anxiety. "We'll never make it, Jesse. Jack said we're supposed to get an early start. He

wanted to be in Wichita early tonight, and tomorrow—"
She broke off, in the face of Jesse's slow outlaw grin.

"They won't leave without us, Angel."

"Oh. No, I suppose not." She smiled, but a wash of heat
tinted her face at the thought of everyone waiting, while
they—

She swallowed. Everyone would know that she and Jesse
had spent the night together.

He was her lover. Her heart tripped an extra beat as the
word formed in her mind. The faces of Jesse's band—
Nancy, Hank, Carlos—flitted, uninvited, into her thoughts.

The anonymity Jesse had bought with this hotel room
was, like the room, for one night only. And if the day clerk
recognized Jesse, even that night would be public knowledge.

She made herself dismiss the thought. What had happened last night had nothing to do with the fact that Jesse
Adam Wilson was a superstar in the music world, or that
women she would never meet had fantasized just the scene
in front of her. Jesse, shirtless, his broad shoulders relaxed, his skilled hands, equally adept at making music and
making love, now resting on her guitar. What had happened between them had to do with something more than
fantasy. More real. And less safe.

He wasn't watching what he played. His dark gaze was
appraising her, his eyebrows raised in a subtle but insistent
question.

For Jesse, she knew, the issue of privacy didn't exist. He
wouldn't care who learned he had slept with her.

Self-conscious, she moved her hands up to her shoulders, resting her elbows on her knees under the sheet. "I can
never get used to hearing someone else play my guitar," she
said, in evasive answer to that look on Jesse's face. "It
sounds different."

He broke off the melody, strummed a couple of chords,
then started again, a different tune. Her own.

The distant gleam of city lights
Was in your eyes today....

He started to sing.

"I know you've got to go
And you know I've got to stay...."

Surprise straightened her back. "That's—note for note.
Just the way I play it."

"Yeah."

"But you've only heard it a couple of times."

"I liked it, though." He played the verse through again,
this time embellishing the line of melody with his own improvisation.

She laughed nervously. "*That's* not the way I play it."

"Nope." He grinned. "It's the way *I* play it."

Her smile faded as she studied him. Realization coalesced in the back of her mind. There were reasons that
Jesse Adam Wilson was a music superstar. He had the kind
of talent that put him two notches above any other musician she'd ever known, and the force of personality that
stamped everything he did with his inimitable style. It was
what kept him invulnerable to the bright, harsh, demanding light of overwhelming success.

Maybe Serita hadn't had such defenses. Maybe she hadn't
had enough talent, enough character. It was a strange and
chilling thought. She had always considered Serita more
talented, more daring, stronger than herself.

Jesse played a line of high notes up on the neck of the
guitar, then broke off and smiled at her. "It's a tune for the
mandolin." He rested his forearm on the curved wooden
edge of the instrument. "I haven't played the mandolin
much lately." He studied her. "It would be nice with your
voice."

She stared back at him, while a knot of warning tightened in her stomach. He assumed he was going to play this with her. A tiny thrill of the panic she thought had been banished the night before shot through her at the thought of Jesse's assumptions.

Whatever he did would be noticed by everyone who listened to this kind of music. Most songwriters would give their eyeteeth to have Jesse sing what they'd written. He could make a career as surely as . . . as he had made Serita's.

But she didn't want Serita's career.

"I'll think about it," she said. She'd meant the comment to sound casual, but even in her own ears she heard the strain in her voice.

Jesse's eyes narrowed slightly, and the black brows drew together in a frown. "You'll think about it," he repeated. She couldn't read the inflection. Still watching her, he lifted the guitar by the neck and set it on the floor, on the other side of him.

"What else are you thinking about, Angel? Last night? You having second thoughts about that?"

"Of course not."

"Good," he said. He didn't smile. "'Cause I'm not takin' it back."

Her mouth twitched but she didn't quite smile. Jesse's hand closed around the shape of her foot under the covers, then slid up to encircle one ankle through the material of the bedspread.

He didn't want a one-night stand. The thought was elating, terrifying and strange. For all her reservations about being a one-night groupie, she had not thought beyond this one anonymous impulsive night.

Jesse moved his hand around to the calf of her leg, massaging it gently, so that the sheet moved against her skin. The covers pulled down from her shoulders. Jesse looked up at her, his gaze darkening.

"Jesse…" Her glance slid toward her watch. "We should get back…. We're going to Kansas…."

"I think there's somethin' we should do here first." With a deft, graceful movement, he slid up beside her on the bed, one hand still on her knee. He moved it along the outline of her thigh, her hip, the curve of her exposed back, then threaded his fingers into her hair. "I haven't had enough of Texas yet."

"Jesse, we can't."

"Yes, we can," he said. His hand, at the back of her neck, exerted gentle pressure to bring her toward him. His mouth touched hers in a kiss that was no less a claim of possession for all its seductive expertise.

Still half-resisting, she lifted her hand to his hair.

"Don't ask me to stop, Angel," he whispered, his mouth at the side of her neck.

The sheet fell away from her shoulders. His hands and his mouth moved on her body, warm as the slanted shaft of sunlight across the bed, until she was melting in his heat, surrendering to the passion he evoked, hers as much as his.

She moved into his arms as he coaxed her down to the mattress and covered her body with his.

And it was Jesse who did the asking, bringing her hands around his neck, coaxing her knees apart with one of his. "Open your eyes, Angel," he demanded gruffly, when her eyelids had fluttered closed and she was lost in sensation. "I want to watch your face when I make love to you, Angel…. I want to see you." And, at the moment of highest passion, "Yes, love, give me that…. Love me, Angel…." She gave him everything in answer, for that moment of Texas splendor.

It was noon when a taxi dropped them off at the hotel where Jesse and his band had been booked. The tour bus was parked in the hotel's driveway, but it was empty. No one from the band was in the lobby either, when Jesse pulled open the glass door and held it for Angel.

"Go ahead and get changed," he told her. "I'll take your guitar." She gave him a brief smile and an uneasy nod. He watched her cross the lobby, her skirt billowing out around her.

The hotel phone was on the front desk. Jesse picked it up, dialed Jack's room number, and said into the receiver, "We're back."

There was almost no pause before Jack replied, "Right," and he hung up.

Fifteen minutes later, when Jesse came down again, the bus was running, the band, except Angel, on it.

Nancy and Tony were sitting in the front section. When Jesse walked by them, carrying the guitar, Tony muttered, "Jack's rippin'." Nancy, her head on Tony's shoulder, made no comment, but her eyes, philosophical and amused, followed him as he passed.

Conversation died as Jesse walked into the back lounge. He crossed to the instrument storage compartments, shelved Angela's guitar, and turned around.

Jack was staring at him, hard. Jesse walked back through the room, past them all, to a seat in the front section.

"She's here," Gil announced from the driver's compartment. He reached for the door lever, grinned at Angel as she put her foot on the step, then closed the door behind her. He had the bus moving before she'd made her way back to the seats. Eyes steady, Jesse watched her.

She'd changed into jeans and a T-shirt, and her expression was wary, nervous and guilty as sin. Her cheek was reddened on one side, where his beard had rubbed against it, her lips slightly swollen. She'd been in his bed less than an hour ago. Jesse's mouth lifted at one corner, but Angel avoided his gaze, and he smiled at her with canny appraisal.

"*Afternoon*, honey," Nancy said, from behind Jesse's head.

Angel's color deepened, but she smiled at Nancy. Jesse watched her gaze flick to the back of the bus, and turned his head that way. Hank was slouched in the doorway to the lounge, smirking at her.

Angel's response to that reaction was telling. She scooted into a seat on the other side of the aisle, put her overnight bag down next to her, and turned to the window.

Jesse let out his breath. He got up, crossed the aisle, tossed her bag onto the seat in front of her, and sat down.

She looked startled.

"Don't let Hank bother you," he said.

"He doesn't—" She broke off. "I'm just not used to living in the spotlight, I guess." She was leaning a little away from him. Her shoulder didn't quite touch his arm, and her eyes didn't quite meet his gaze. She was having second thoughts about living in the spotlight. Where he was.

"Get used to it."

She looked into his eyes.

"There's going to be a lot of publicity, with the benefit concert," he said bluntly. He didn't give her a chance to answer. And he didn't intend to give her a chance to back away from him. Not after last night. He couldn't have stopped himself then, and he couldn't let her go now. "People are bound to talk, you being Rita's cousin," he said. "You don't have to listen if it bothers you. Eventually they'll find someone else to talk about."

"But I—" She hesitated. "But we—"

Jesse could see a wash of panic in her face, like the nervousness she exuded whenever she thought she wouldn't be able to handle one of the audiences who ended up eating out of her hand and clamoring for more. Her eyes were as wary as a trapped kitten's. "We what?" he said.

"We don't have to give people a lot to talk about, Jesse. We can be a little circumspect, can't we?"

"No. We can't. Be a little circumspect." He gave the word a derisive twist. "What do you want me to do? Sneak around to your room after-hours? Pretend I'm room service?"

She looked away.

"I know what it takes to cover something up to the press, Angel. It takes a hell of a lot of deception. A hell of a lot of lies. And in the end it changes how you feel about it."

Another flush of color tinted her cheekbones. Her mouth was set in a straight line, as if she were holding it against showing any expression. Against letting herself feel anything.

Jesse exhaled a long history of experience. "How many times do you think I can spend the night in your room before some hotel bellhop notices?"

She said tightly, still not looking at him, "Maybe you're taking a lot for granted."

His eyes narrowed. He wasn't going to let her go. He reached up to her face and ran the back of his knuckle down her cheek, where the skin was pink. "What is it I shouldn't be taking for granted?"

She pulled away. Her glance skittered to Tony and Nancy, behind them and across the aisle. Both were watching the public exchange. Roughly, with sudden intensity, Jesse slid his hand around her neck, pulled her toward him, and tipped her chin up with his free hand. Her lips parted in surprise and she gazed at his face, the expression in her wide gray-green eyes vulnerable, scared, bright with threatened tears. She caught her lower lip between her teeth.

Jesse let her go, and she turned back toward the window and propped her elbow on the sill. Her hand, at the side of her head, was trembling.

He had almost made her cry. And it made him feel like a bastard. Angry at himself, he settled back against the seat, then let out another long breath and glanced at her.

"I put your guitar in the back, Angel," he said neutrally.

She didn't look at him. "Thank you."

"It's in one of the storage compartments, if you want it."

"All right."

He studied her a moment. "I . . . thought you might want to play it, work out some more stuff. I've got the mandolin."

The blond hair brushed her shoulder as she shook her head. "No."

"No, what?"

She dropped her elbow from the windowsill and turned toward him. "No mandolin," she said deliberately.

He frowned. "You want to try it with just the harp?"

"No. It's already tried. I'll play the song with Hank and Carlos."

"Angel—"

"No," she said again, defensively, quickly.

Frustration coiled in the pit of his stomach. "What the hell is that going to prove, Angel?"

"I'm not trying to prove anything, *dammit*!" Her voice rose on the sentence, high-pitched and thin, and a catch that was almost a sob was in the last word. She looked again at Nancy and Tony, who were looking back at them with half-concealed curiosity, then she put her hand over her face and bent her head down.

Jesse had an angry, frustrated urge to snatch her wrist away from her face, turn her toward him and kiss her, no matter who was watching, as he'd almost done a moment ago.

He swore under his breath, pulled himself up from the seat and stalked back to the lounge.

Jack was sitting at the bar, leaning on the upholstered edge, his coffee cup in front of him. He gave Jesse an angry look, his shoulders stiff.

Frank and Carlos were in the corner, playing cards. Beside them, Hank was sprawled on one of the sofas, Jesse's Gibson across his lap. He was picking out a tune with his index finger, plucking the strings as if he were playing his bass. He let the melody drift off as Jesse crossed the lounge, scowling, and sat at the other end of the sofa.

Hank's glance moved from Jesse to the neck of the guitar. He flicked a finger against the eagle-feather necklace to set it swinging, then grinned at Jesse. "I hear Serita's benefit concert's been rescheduled."

"Yeah."

"Since when?"

"Since yesterday morning."

Hank picked another line of notes. "Ah do declare. News surely does travel fast in this band."

Jesse reached for the neck of the guitar, yanked it out of Hank's hands, and leaned it against the corner of the sofa.

Jack picked up his coffee cup. His gaze was still steady and expressionless, on Jesse.

"You gonna let us know when it is?" Hank drawled, looking at Jesse.

"Two weeks from yesterday."

Hank shrugged, eyebrows raised, processing the information. "So we have a week's vacation in sunny South Dakota before the gig."

Jack's hard stare moved toward Hank. "There are some contingencies to this benefit," he said shortly. "If there's any trouble in town during that week, the concert's canceled. There's been a lot of bad feelings between Indians and whites around there since Rita's death. Any sign they're being stirred up and the promoters will cut this off cold. And they're going to be keeping a sharp eye on things in Wichita and Lincoln, too. Everything's got to happen right for the next few bookings."

Hank grunted.

Jack's sharp gaze moved to Jesse. "And it would help," he said caustically, "if we got there on time."

Jesse shot Jack a brief look and pulled his hat down over his forehead. He said nothing.

Jack stared at him. "I stuck my neck out pretty far to get this concert booked. I made a lot of promises that won't mean squat next time if we don't deliver now."

Jesse met his eyes, still silent.

"One of them was that Angel Trent was opening the performance. If she doesn't show because she can't handle it, you're gonna have one hell of a lot of explanations to come up with."

The bus's engine growled rhythmically as Gil pulled into the passing lane, trying to make up lost time. Jesse squared his shoulders against the back of the couch, then pushed himself up from it and crossed the lounge toward Jack. He got out a mug and poured coffee into it, then stood, one shoulder against the wall, his gaze on his manager as he swallowed a mouthful of coffee.

Hank reached across the sofa for the guitar and started to play it again.

"I'll do my best not to mess up the girl, Jack," Jesse said.

"I *thought* you were going to leave her alone." Jack's voice was low and even.

Jesse set the mug down on the bar with a sharp click. "I tried."

"Not—hard—enough."

"I'm not a saint."

"You want me to believe she seduced you?" Jack said, sarcasm in his voice.

"I want you to believe she's not going to get hurt."

"Right." Jack nodded, his eyes narrowed. "And you want me to believe she can handle everything. You, this benefit, the kind of trouble that's likely to come up in Yankton Rapids—"

"You said it yourself, Jack. She's done a damn good job of every concert we've had."

"This is different."

Jesse met his stony glare.

"I don't have to tell you it's different. The media is going to be all over her, Jesse. She's Rita's cousin, for God's sake."

"I know that."

"Then why the hell didn't you remember it last night?"

Jesse was silent.

"You've got a hell of a selective memory when there's something you want, don't you?"

Jesse made his jaw unclench. In the corner, Hank strummed a chord on the Gibson.

"It's done, Jack. No point in talking about it."

"How about the benefit?" Jack said succinctly. "Any point in talking about that?"

"She can handle it."

Jack stared at him.

"I'm telling you she'll sing."

Jack nodded skeptically, irritation and disgust evident in the gesture.

Jesse turned away from him. He let his gaze rest for a moment on Hank, then he looked back at the manager, studying the big Irishman. He pushed himself away from the wall, leaned over the bar, his weight on his palms, and said, "I want to open the concert with her, Jack. With the band."

"No."

"It would work. I know it would work, and she—"

"No!" He slammed his hands down on the bar and stood up, making Jesse straighten, nose to nose with him. "She's consistently refused to perform with the band. She doesn't want to be a country-western phenomenon, she doesn't want anybody mixing her up with her Serita and she doesn't want to perform under the kind of pressure you make, Jesse. And you have no right to ask that of her."

"Why not?"

"Because you took her to bed, you bastard." He leaned closer to Jesse, his chin thrust out belligerently.

Jesse stared back. "That subject's closed—" he said.

"No, it isn't. Back off about the music, Jesse."

"Dammit!" He jammed his hands into his pockets. "What would y'have me do? Leave her alone to play *folk music* for a while, and then go home to Nebraska when she decides she can't measure up to her cousin? You said yourself we need her for Rita's concert. You think leaving her alone last night would have gotten her up on that stage?"

"You think taking her to bed *will*?"

"Yes."

Jack's gaze shifted suddenly as he straightened, looking over Jesse's shoulder.

Jesse turned around.

Angel was standing in the doorway, watching them, her face a careful mask of indifference. But the gray-green eyes were anything but indifferent. Shock, hurt and vulnerability were as visible and unguarded as the passion she'd shown so freely just an hour before.

She looked around the room, her gaze stopping on Jack, Carlos, Hank—then the eagle-feather necklace hanging from Jesse's guitar.

Her mouth worked, but without a sound she turned on her heel and disappeared through the doorway.

"Angel—" Jesse took a step toward the door. Jack's big hand, on his elbow, stopped him.

"Better let it ride, Jess," the manager said. "You'll just make it worse."

Jesse shook off his arm, muttered a graphic epithet and jammed his hat down on his head. He turned and followed Angel out to the front of the bus.

Eight

Angel was sitting by the window with her overnight bag next to her, her hand on it.

"This seat's taken," she said through clenched teeth when Jesse stopped beside her.

"You want me to stand in the aisle?"

She looked up at him. The emotion he'd seen so often just below the surface was nakedly visible in those green eyes—hurt, resentment, anger. "I want you to drop dead, Jesse Wilson," she said. "Preferably onstage, in front of every groupie who ever thought you were worth mooning over and everyone on this bus who ever heard you bragging about your *not-so-private* conquests."

Guilt shot through him. "Angel..." He gestured, palm up. "Look, it's an old argument with Jack."

"Well I guess you won it, didn't you?"

"No, I didn't win it." He looked away from her pale, tense face. He made himself look back. "Jack thinks I'm a bastard."

"So do I."

His glance dropped to the overnight bag beside her. "Can I sit down?"

"No."

"Angel, I just want—"

"I know what you *want*. I overheard it, remember? You want to make sure I open for Serita's benefit." Her voice was low, but edged with emotion. "Is that what you had in mind last night? Was that in the back of your mind all the time you were telling me that no one was thinking about Serita?"

"No." He jerked the bag out of her hand and sat down beside her, facing her in the seat. "No one was thinking about Serita last night. If there was anything in my mind at all, it was that maybe you ought to go back to your hotel room by yourself and—"

"And heed your warning?" Her eyes glinted. The tears were close to the surface. "Yes, I should have. It was the one thing you said that might indicate you have a conscience."

"Angel..." He jerked his hat down on his forehead, then looked at her again. "Maybe it was true, but—"

"Maybe it was true. There isn't any maybe about it. You don't even bother to lie, do you? You get everything you want, anyway."

He felt himself flinch. It was what Jack had said. How long had she been standing there? He swore under his breath. "I didn't mean for you to hear that."

"No, I bet you didn't," she said with a cynicism that cut into his conscience.

"Listen to me, Angel," he said, his voice rough and urgent. "I'm running this tour. It's my job to make sure it goes right, to make it work."

"Well, you certainly were very good at your job last night." She stared at him for a silent, hurtful moment, her chin raised, her eyes a little too defiant. Then she turned her head sharply toward the window, away from Jesse.

Without thought, he reached for her and snapped her face around toward him. His thumb pressed into the curve of her jaw, demanding and entreating. Almost unconsciously, he moved it in a slow, shaky caress. "It wasn't like that last night, Angel. You know it wasn't."

"Don't." She ran out of voice on the word. Her lower lip was trembling, and the brightness of her eyes had spilled over into two tears at the corners.

He let out a long breath, and dropped his hand. She looked out the window at the passing Amarillo landscape. He pushed himself up from the seat, stood in the aisle a moment, then glanced toward the lounge door. Nancy's eyes, resigned but sympathetic, met his.

He turned and walked the other way, toward the driver's compartment.

"Gil." he barked.

"Yeah."

"Pull over at the next rest area. I'll drive."

Gil glanced at him, then looked back to the road, silent. Five minutes later he pulled off. "You know where we're going?" he asked Jesse as he took over the seat.

"Yeah. South Dakota."

The roadie shook his head as he moved from the compartment. "Well, see if you can hit Wichita on the way, will ya?"

The bus growled through the gears as Jesse pulled out onto the highway.

Three nights later Angel sat in a motel room in Yankton Rapids, South Dakota, staring at four bland white walls and a picture window that opened onto a parking lot.

The town beyond the parking lot had a Grange hall, a tractor dealership, a marginally solvent, marginally tacky business district, and sixteen bars. There were two hospitals: Memorial, at one end of town, and the Bureau of Indian Affairs Clinic at the other end.

Serita had died at Memorial.

Beyond the hospital grounds, within sight of it, was the ball field where the benefit concert was scheduled for five days later.

The thought of it made the tendons in her neck tense with a now-familiar panic.

In Wichita, Jesse had been reckless, unrestrained and volatile. The audience had stood on the seats and screamed themselves hoarse. She had left before the end of the concert, walking out past Jack's set and angry face as the manager watched Jesse's act from backstage.

In Lincoln, the crowd had been primed by Wichita reviews. They'd been boisterous and restive even before she'd gone on. She'd refused to do the song she'd worked out with Hank and Carlos. She hadn't wanted the audience's reaction to it. If they'd taken it as a signal to drop whatever restraint they had, she would have lost control of them. The thought of handling a crowd whipped into the mood that Jesse elicited at will made her palms grow clammy and her stomach turn over in fear.

She'd stuck to folk music and they'd accepted it, grudgingly, with a few shouted requests for something faster. She'd ignored the requests, just as she'd ignored Jesse's hard, disbelieving appraisal of her conservative, restrained performance.

He'd stopped her as she walked off, and turned her around, both hands on her shoulders, to make her look at him. "Wait for me after the concert, Angel," he'd said.

The rough entreaty in his voice had touched her senses with a chord of response she hadn't wanted, but couldn't silence. Against all reason, her heart had started to beat faster.

She hadn't waited.

Not then, at the theater.

She glanced around again at the bland motel room, then let out a defeated sigh. It seemed she'd done nothing but wait since then.

Her eyes moved restlessly to the phone, but there was no one she could call. Everyone in the band—even Jack—had gone out. She had a rental car parked outside the room, but she didn't have the faintest idea of any place to go.

And if she ran into Jesse...

She knew what would happen if she ran into Jesse. He would talk, he would persuade, he would touch her. And she would forgive him.

She tipped her head back, closing her eyes. The longing for his touch was so intense it was an ache. The conflict of emotion and logic was a knot at the center of her chest.

All reason told her she should resist, should keep her distance. But she knew if she let herself listen to him, be with him, she would forgive him. She would forgive anything for the exquisite pleasure of his touch.

And she would get hurt again.

Jesse Wilson scowled down at the jukebox in the Red Hawk Café. There wasn't anything on it he wanted to hear, but he needed the noise. The bar was smoky, dim and crowded with strangers, Indian and white, all of them vocal and uninhibited under the influence of alcohol. Still there wasn't noise enough to take his mind off a Nebraska folksinger with hair like pale sunlight and eyes as vulnerable as new growth on a Texas prairie. And she thought he was a bastard.

He drank another mouthful of beer, examined the bottle and contemplated trading it in for whiskey. If he'd been drinking whiskey, it wouldn't matter what was on the damn jukebox.

As long as it wasn't by him. He wasn't in the mood to listen to his own voice. He'd left the rest of his band at the bar down the street because he wasn't fit company for anyone he knew.

There was a booth full of construction workers next to him. One of them craned his neck over the booth, watching Jesse, then called, "Play H-7, if ya don't know what ya want."

Jesse glanced at him indifferently, then looked back at the selections list. H-7 was a recent oldie: "Hope and Dreams." By Serita Black. The Red Hawk Café had been her turf. The jukebox had half a dozen of her songs listed.

He hadn't heard any of them for more than a year.

He stared at the title, in small black capital letters, wondering what he felt. There was a time when any reference to Serita's music would have eaten at his gut like acid. Now some of the edges were blunted, some of the bitter, cold rage was dulled.

On impulse, he raised a hand, stabbed at the numbers with an index finger, and turned his back on the machine.

A young woman in tight jeans and a well-filled sweater crossed in front of him, to a chorus of whistles and suggestions from the booth. She gave Jesse a smile and headed for a corner of the bar, where she stood waiting for the bartender, pretending to be unaware of any male scrutiny. Jesse watched her, eyes hooded. She wasn't bad. His type, he thought cynically. Not too young, willing, well-enough traveled.

He walked back to his place at the other end of the bar, still watching the girl. "Whiskey," he said shortly as the bartender went by him on his way to take her order.

The whiskey appeared in front of him on the return trip. The bartender in the Red Hawk didn't keep his customers waiting. Jesse reached for his wallet, and the bartender shook his head. "This one's on the lady," he said, nodding toward the end of the bar. Jesse glanced at her, fingering the whiskey glass, wondering how hard it would be to make himself believe she was an angel with pale sunlight hair and smoky green eyes, in a hotel room in Amarillo.

The girl in the sweater picked up her drink, walked around the corner of the bar toward him and crossed behind him, close enough so that the side of her breast brushed his arm when she sat down next to him. He held his glass up toward her and swallowed the contents.

The whiskey was raw and strong. It burned in his stomach as the first strains of Serita's husky, hard voice poured out of the jukebox.

All I am is hope and dreams.
Tryin' to live on lies and schemes...

"What the hell is this?" a slurred voice said in his other ear. "Sacred to the memory of Serita Black?"

Jesse turned his head. The dark-eyed, high-cheekboned face sneering back at him belonged to someone he knew.

Luke Standing Horse slid onto the bar stool next to Jesse's, flipped his head to brush a shock of straight, black hair out of his eyes and set his bottle down on the bar. He was wearing a blue work shirt and threadbare cords that hung loosely on his tall frame. He was thinner than Jesse remembered him, his face lined at the corners of the mouth in a way he didn't recall seeing when Luke had been with Serita.

Jesse's hand dropped, unconsciously, to the Navaho buckle at his own belt. "Evening, Luke," he said.

The black eyes bored into his for a moment. "I don't care for your taste in music," the Indian said offensively. "I don't like oldies."

Jesse's mouth thinned. "I didn't know you were listening."

I know that what we had was real,
I know the way it made me feel...

Luke turned his head toward the bartender and lifted his chin. The man brought over another beer. Jesse gazed at the Indian. He and Luke had never smiled at each other much, but the black sneer that darkened Luke's face now wasn't what he remembered, either.

The Indian reached for the bottle and raised it to his mouth. He swallowed half the beer, then let the bottle hang carelessly from his fingers. His eyes slid toward the girl behind Jesse's shoulder. "Find yourself some easy tail, Jesse?"

The girl banged her drink down on the bar, stood up and shot Luke a furious look. Her gaze moved to Jesse, then she turned her back on them. She hesitated long enough to let Jesse know she was willing to be placated, but he didn't make the gesture, and she stalked off in the direction of the booths.

"Where's your *girlfriend* tonight?" Luke sneered. "The blond Angel?"

Jesse didn't answer him, and Luke laughed cynically. "She anything like her cousin?" he asked, his voice taunting. "Keep you busy at night? Or is she out keeping someone else busy?"

The muscle in Jesse's jaw clenched. His eyes hardened into cold, black granite. "Keep your mouth shut about Angel, Luke. And keep it shut about Rita, too, while you're at it."

"You're the one played the song, man."

"Maybe I wanted to hear it."

Luke leaned toward Jesse, contempt evident in the lines of his body. "Rita's dead," he drawled, as if he sensed that another mention of Angel would trip the last of Jesse's control. "She's become one of the ancestral spirits, in the great Sioux religion. Shooting coke in the happy hunting grounds. I'd just as soon not hear her voice."

The muscle in Jesse's jaw clenched tighter. "That's your business," he said.

Luke drank again. "And what's your business, Wilson? Benefit concerts? Give the Injuns somethin' to remember their princess by?"

Slowly Jesse turned on the bar stool. Rita's voice was a low, throbbing ache of melody from the speaker on the jukebox.

"You need something to remember her by, Luke?"

"No, man," the Indian said bitterly. "I got no use for memories. I got all the memories I need." His mouth curled. "'Specially 'bout a drugged-out, dime-store—"

"Shut up," Jesse said. He didn't move or raise his voice, but the words were dangerous.

Luke twisted around, his body facing Jesse, one hand still on his beer. "You gonna make me?"

Jesse stared at Luke for a long, silent moment, the muscles of his shoulders and neck drawn up in tension, while the whiskey in his stomach burned again, like acid. His hand closed into a fist but the control held. Slowly he shook his head. "No."

"Why not?"

"Because you're drunk."

The Indian stood up, finished his beer and set the bottle on the bar.

Love is never what it seems...

Luke's face turned slightly toward the jukebox, then the hard, flat gaze swung back to Jesse. "I may be drunk, but at least I ain't the one that's dead," he said. He turned and stalked toward the door. As he passed the jukebox he stopped, reached behind it and yanked out the cord. The music died abruptly, and there was an angry, belligerent chorus of protest from the bar.

Luke disappeared out the door as two of the construction workers shoved their way out of the booth, swearing at him, obviously spoiling for a fight.

The bartender got to the door before the customers. "All right, boys. Take it easy." He blocked the door and kept talking. "No harm done. Sit down, now. We don't want any cops here tonight." He was big, well muscled and experienced. The potential fight dwindled to a belligerent murmur and the men at the door reluctantly went back to their seats.

The bartender plugged in the jukebox and produced a quarter for it.

"You want to hear the song again?" he said to Jesse. "Your choice." There were shouted comments from the clientele, but he ignored them, looking at Jesse.

"No," Jesse said. "Play whatever you want." He turned back to his beer, his mood violent and black.

His *choice* was in a motel room playing folk music and drinking tea, trying to pretend that what had been between them was erasable.

Gone.

Love is never what it seems, I never get it right

Rita again sang from the jukebox.

"Whiskey," he muttered again when the bartender returned.

The man brought it, set it down in front of Jesse, then said softly, as if he were reading Jesse's mood, "I don't stand for no trouble here. Not from no one."

Jesse's eyes bored into him and his mouth hardened. The bartender moved away, unsmiling.

Before the song changed on the jukebox the empty bar stool beside Jesse was occupied again.

"Howdy," a tall, slick-voiced cowboy said to him, smiling.

Jesse scowled at the man. He had an expensive leather jacket, reddish hair that hung lank under a Stetson that could only have come from Texas, and something in his voice that grated on Jesse's nerves.

"You're Jesse Adam Wilson, ain't ya."

"Yeah."

The man nodded, then sipped from his drink. Ice cubes clinked in spiked orange juice in a tall glass with a sprig of mint on the side.

"I got something you might be int'rested in," the slick voice said.

Jesse glanced at him again. Beside him, like an entourage, was a dark-haired thug with a morose face, and a thin, black-clad Mexican. "I doubt it," Jesse said.

The redhead chuckled. His laugh had a greasy sound. "Look at this." With a smug smile at his companions, he reached inside his jacket, pulled out a handful of long, white-tipped feathers, and dropped them on the bar beside Jesse's beer.

Jesse stared at them while his jaw slowly tightened, and he turned his head toward the redhead. Memory coalesced in the back of his mind: a phone call from someone named Red, the offer to sell Indian artifacts....

"You know what they are?" the man asked, grinning.

Jesse didn't answer him.

"They're money, in the right hands, Jesse."

Jesse's silence stretched out, dangerous and explosive. The speaker made the mistake of ignoring it.

"I got the whole bird. It was shot by a gen-u-ine Injun, on the reservation. And there's more where—"

Jesse's fist shot out and connected with the redhead's jaw. His head snapped back and his body hit the edge of the bar, knocking his orange drink onto the floor.

The thug behind him took one practiced step forward and slammed his fist into Jesse's stomach. Air exploded from Jesse's lungs. He found his footing, braced an elbow on the bar, and kicked the thug's knees out from under him. The man's second punch grazed Jesse's shoulder, deflected.

"Hey!" There was a strident shout from someone in the bar. Bodies started moving toward them. Out of the corner of his eye, Jesse saw the bartender reach for the wall phone.

The redhead had righted himself on the stool. Beside him, the thin Mexican spun around and slammed a fist into the side of Jesse's head.

Stars exploded in the space behind Jesse's eyes. He staggered backward toward the door. Through the haze, he saw the Mexican knocked against the bar.

Someone he didn't know swung at him. He ducked, braced himself, and came up with his fist in the man's face.

The bar had erupted into a full-scale brawl. A glass beside Jesse smashed on the floor. Beer ran under his feet.

The thug who'd hit him first pushed his way toward Jesse and landed another punch to the solar plexus. Blind rage made Jesse swing back, fighting with unmeditated instinct, while around him the grunts and shouts of the bar's patrons were punctuated with the thud of bodies on furniture and the smashing of glass. Another fist slammed into the side of his mouth. A shock of pain deadened his jaw. He tasted blood. Someone else was swinging toward him. He blocked the fist with his forearm, but a kick caught him in the ribs. Half-conscious, he heard police sirens.

Behind him, there was a scuffle, the shouted demands of the police and more breaking glass. Jesse ducked another blow. He glimpsed the bartender shoving his way into the brawl, swinging a sawed-off baseball bat.

A hand closed around Jesse's shoulder and hauled him back. He spun around, swung from the shoulder, and felt his fist connect with the jaw of one of Yankton Rapids's finest. The blue-uniformed cop beside the one Jesse had hit came up at him with a nightstick. There was a dull thud, an explosion of pain and a dizzying haze.

Thirty seconds later he was thrust up against the wall of the bar, his hands yanked behind him and the feel of cold metal on his wrists. The handcuffs clicked shut, someone jerked his arm and Jesse stumbled out in the direction he was pulled.

There was yet another voice in his ear, this one reading him his rights. The door of the police car was pulled open and Jesse was shoved in. He leaned his head gingerly back against the seat, closed his eyes, and elected to remain silent.

The phone in Angel's motel room shrilled. She jumped, startled, and stared at it for a moment before she got up to answer it.

"Angel—" Jesse's voice said. It sounded muffled and thick.

"Jesse?"

There was a silence.

"Jesse?" she said again.

"Yeah." In the background she could hear voices, doors opening and closing, someone typing erratically. "I'm at the police station," he said, in that same thick voice. "Come bail me out."

"You're in...jail?" Incredulity lifted her voice at the end of the question.

"Bail's a hundred dollars."

The statement was peremptory, the request given as an order. Emotions rippled through her: disbelief, a surge of anger, a driving need to know what had happened, and the ironic sense of being inexorably caught in a trap she couldn't spring. For the past two days she had planned how to resist whatever request he might make of her. But she hadn't anticipated this one.

She closed her eyes and took a deep breath. "I'll...be there."

There was another silence, then Jesse said brusquely, "Thanks," and the connection went dead.

She knew where the police station was. She'd driven by it in her tour of Yankton Rapids. She had—barely—a hundred dollars.

And as of now, she thought wryly, she had a place to go.

It was a short trip. She walked into the concrete-block building, her shoulders squared and her expression carefully neutral, stopped at the desk inside the door and said to the young policeman who looked up at her, "I want to bail someone out."

"Yeah," the young man said, reaching for a stack of forms on the corner of the desk.

"His name is—"

"Yeah, I know what his name is." He glanced up at her. "You're Angel Trent, huh?"

She gazed back at him, her eyes opened a little wider. "Yes," she said.

"Bail's a hundred dollars," he said sourly. "He assaulted a police officer."

Shock kept her silent for a moment, then her shoulders slumped. She glanced down to her handbag and fumbled with her wallet.

"Wait here, Miss Trent." The young officer stood up, walked toward the back room and said something to another uniformed man behind a desk. A chair scraped back. From the empty desk in front of her, a CB monitor crackled with a garbled report. The room smelled of dust, sweat and disinfectant.

She had never in her life been in a police station. She had no defense against the undeniable feeling of intimidation it brought out. The air seemed charged with a tough and inviolable division: police and criminals. And because of Jesse Adam Wilson, she felt as if she were on the wrong side of the lineup.

A metal door squeaked open, then banged shut again. Jesse walked through the doorway.

He held a washcloth to the corner of his mouth, his knuckles ragged and scraped. Over one eye was a swelling, purple bruise. His shirt gaped open where two buttons had been torn off the front, and he reeked of beer.

The clipped, no-nonsense greeting she'd rehearsed in her mind was lost in the remembered words of her grandfather's favorite oath. "Sweet Lord," she muttered.

The uncovered half of Jesse's mouth curved up in a grin that held no humor.

"Would you sign this, please, Mr. Wilson?" the young policeman asked. Under the conventional courtesy was the hard contempt of a cop in a town where the cops were too often challenged to be lenient.

Jesse didn't seem to notice. He bent over the desk and took the offered pen. His bruised fingers closed awkwardly around it. He signed.

"And, Miss Trent—"

She pulled her gaze away from Jesse to the form she was expected to sign. The policeman's hard, contemptuous stare was turned toward her. She was guilty, she understood, by association. Color rose in her face. In spite of her rationalizations, she felt seamy, sordid and somehow tainted by her part in this. She took the pen, silently cursing Jesse Adam Wilson, and scrawled her name, but when she turned back to him, her stomach tightened at the sight of his battered face. She reached instinctively for his arm.

He glanced down at her outstretched hand, then the dark gaze flicked back to hers. "I can walk," he said.

She swallowed the rejection, pulled her arm back, but didn't move until Jesse put a hand on the middle of her spine and ushered her toward the door.

They got into the car and Angel pulled away from the curb in silence. A block from the station, she took a breath and glanced at him. "What . . . happened?"

"I got arrested." The words were sharp with finality.

He took the washcloth away from his face. It was covered with blood. His lip had been cut at the corner.

The car slowed almost to a halt as Angel stared at him in alarm. "Should I take you to a hospital?"

"No."

She continued to stare.

"You want me to drive?" he asked shortly.

A surge of anger straightened her spine and snapped her head around to the road. "I don't think you'd better. When you ask me to bail you out for being charged with drunk driving, I won't be able to. I'm out of money."

Jesse said nothing. He put the washcloth back to his mouth.

In spite of her fury, she felt herself flinch when it touched his lip. Her stomach was churning with conflicting emotions: resentment and anger juxtaposed against concern and fresh hurt at Jesse's rejection. Tears welled behind her eyes and she fought them back.

She realized just after she'd passed it that she'd missed the turn to their motel.

Jesse took the cloth away from his mouth and jerked his head toward her.

"I *know*," she snapped at him.

Her voice was high-pitched, shaded with hysteria. She clamped her mouth shut and turned the car around.

They didn't speak while she drove to the motel and pulled into the driveway.

"I'm in thirty-two A," Jesse said.

It was the opposite wing of the motel from her own room. She had to stop again, back around and cross the parking lot. She did it bristling with defensiveness, hearing disapproval in his silence. Did he expect her to know where his room was? She bit her lip, hard enough to stop the tears that still threatened.

She stopped in front of unit thirty-two A, staring straight ahead of her at the windshield, waiting for Jesse to get out.

He didn't move. When she glanced at him finally, he was looking back at her, the dark eyes searching her face.

"Thanks," he said, the word gruff but so soft it was barely audible.

She bit down on her lip again as the tears, unwanted but too close to the surface to be checked forever, filled her eyes.

Some expression crossed Jesse's face that wrenched at her volatile emotions.

"I shouldn't have asked you to do this." he said. "It's not anything that's ever been part of your life. I had no right to drag you into it. I'm sorry."

She swallowed the lump in her throat and blinked hard, staring down at her lap. "There wasn't anyone else to call, was there? Everyone else was out." Her tear-brightened gaze met his, then skittered off.

"I could've stayed in jail. I've done it before." He gave a self-deprecating chuckle. "This time, though, Jack might've left me there."

She hadn't thought she could smile, but something tugged at the corners of her mouth. She looked back at him. "I suppose he might have."

Under the brim of his hat, his eyes appraised her steadily. "I'm glad you were here," he said.

The words were unadorned and his expression was unreadable. The purple bruise at his temple was more swelled than it had been. His lip was bleeding again.

"Can I—" She broke off the offer, not wanting it to be rejected, but it wasn't in her to withhold help so obviously needed, and she took a breath and started again. "Can I get you anything?"

There was another silence, then Jesse said, "I could use a cup of coffee. Maybe the office would have some."

She glanced at him, nodded, and swallowed again.

"I'll be in the shower," Jesse said. He got out of the car and slammed the door shut.

Angel drove across the parking lot, bought two cups of black coffee from the office machine and took them back to Jesse's room. The shower was running when she walked in.

She set the Styrofoam cups down on the night table, then stood uncertainly in the middle of the room, gazing at the closed bathroom door, her car keys still in her hand.

She should leave now. She glanced down at the keys, jiggling the ring, then looked around the room. It was identical to hers—bland, clean, comfortable. Beside the phone were some scribbled notes about technical equipment. Two packages of guitar strings had been tossed on the bed. Jesse's mandolin case was on the floor, unlatched. There was a mandolin pick on the dented pillow. She smiled ruefully and she sat down on the edge of the bed.

The water stopped running. There was a short span of quiet, then, abruptly, the bathroom door opened. Jesse was shirtless, in jeans. His hair was wet and moisture glistened on the dark hair at the center of his chest. His lip was swelled but had stopped bleeding. When he daubed at it with a corner of the towel that hung around his neck, the terry cloth came off clean.

He let the corners of the towel drop.

"I've got coffee," she said, with a nervous gesture toward the night table.

He crossed the room, picked up a cup and pried the lid off, then sat down beside her on the bed. He leaned forward, elbows on his knees, letting his head droop. "It's been a hell of a night," he said, his voice ragged.

"What happened?"

He glanced at her, then looked down again. For a moment, she thought he wouldn't answer, and another stab of pain shot through her.

"I was in the Red Hawk," Jesse said.

"A bar?"

He looked at her. "Yeah." He looked down at his coffee cup. "One of Serita's old haunts. There was a guy there named Luke Standing Horse. He was Serita's—'' He broke off, glancing at her again. ''Her lover,'' Jesse continued softly. ''He loved her. I know he did. And he believed in what she was doing—Indian pride, education—''

Jesse let out a slow breath and drank a mouthful of coffee. ''He was drunk tonight. Drunk and ticked off at the world. He didn't like the song I played on the jukebox.''

A cold sense of inevitability snaked up her spine. She knew which song it must have been. She crossed her arms in front of her, cupping her elbows in her hands. ''One of Serita's songs?'' she asked.

Jesse nodded. ''He didn't like memories, didn't believe in ancestral spirits. He was talking like he thought it was all nonsense—the benefit, the Indian thing—mouthing off about Rita, about—'' Jesse broke off abruptly and gave her a quick, veiled look.

Another cold shiver prickled at the back of her neck. About you, Jesse had almost said. She had a swift, chilling image of herself being drawn, inevitably, inexorably, into something alien and sordid. Police stations. Barroom conversations. Drunken insinuations.

She couldn't handle this. It was Serita's world Jesse was describing, not hers. Serita's turf. She squeezed her eyes shut for a moment.

Had her cousin sat in the Red Hawk with her Indian lover? Gone there to meet a drug dealer? Bought the cocaine that had killed her?

Serita hadn't been able to handle it either, had she?

Her eyes opened and her wary, apprehensive gaze moved to Jesse's cut and swelled lip.

He raised one hand to it in reflex, then dropped his arm and closed both his fists around the coffee cup. ''I didn't hit him,'' Jesse said. ''But the next guy that spoke to me wanted to sell me a dead eagle. He said it was shot on the reservation. I figured *he* was worth hitting.''

She stared at him, trying to understand the story, trying to fathom her tangled feelings about it. "But at the station, they said you assaulted a police officer."

Jesse gave her another look, his grin made lopsided by the swelled cut. "I didn't know he was a cop until after I hit him."

"What?"

"It was a brawl, Angel. Everyone got into it. I didn't know who I was hitting."

He glanced at her face again, then shook his head in a dismissive gesture. "The boys in the bar were lookin' for a fight. When Luke Standing Horse left, he yanked out the plug to the jukebox, and they would've kicked his teeth in then if the bartender hadn't stopped it."

He rubbed the bridge of his nose between thumb and forefinger, then drank again from the coffee cup.

Angel watched him, confusion and incredulity keeping her silent. When he glanced at her his mouth curved sourly over the cup. "It's a bar, Angel."

She looked away from him, down at her lap. "They were going to beat someone up over a song on the j-jukebox?" Her voice shook on the last words.

"It's a rough town," Jesse said gently.

The cold chill had spread all through her body, along with the sense of alienation. She was entangled in something she couldn't fathom. She twisted her hands together to keep them from shaking. "Will...the concert be called off?" she asked, still not looking at Jesse.

There was a still, hard pause. "Not if I can help it."

Her gaze flew up to his face. It was set and grim and determined.

Fear coursed through her. *Jesse was part of this.* She'd been right about him in the first place. He was ruthless. Ruthless and hard, and as rough and ungovernable as the town he'd just described.

She didn't belong here.

"Don't go," Jesse said. The words were spoken before she'd made a move, as if he sensed her intentions.

Jolted by the sense that he could read her thoughts, she forced herself to hold his gaze, and summoned a flicker of defiant anger.

"Please," Jesse said.

It was so quiet it was barely a gruff murmur. She felt her anger dissolving, like clay, into something softer, something infinitely more vulnerable.

He reached toward her and caught a lock of her hair between his fingers. He folded it gently, examining the texture, then let it fall. He fanned her hair behind her shoulder with the back of his knuckles. His hand slid down her back, under her hair, and he leaned toward her. His lips, uneven and bruised, touched hers. His tongue flicked along the opening of her mouth. She tasted coffee, clean shower water, the faintly bitter tang of blood.

Behind him, he put the coffee cup down.

"Jesse..." She pulled her head back, but her hands, raised to his shoulders to push him away, made no move except a slow, telling grip around the hard, honed muscles. "I don't want to, Jesse...."

He silenced her with a finger against her mouth, trailed his fingertip down over her chin and the soft skin of her throat, then skimmed his hand down the row of buttons on her shirt. "Maybe you don't want to, Angel, but you do...." he said just before he kissed her again.

Want him? or love him? He didn't finish the statement.

It didn't matter. It was true either way. She let her hands slide around his naked back; let her tongue meet his in a touch that was exquisitely gentle, explosively erotic; let him love her until the rich, oblivious melting of her senses washed out all other voices in her mind.

Nine

The yellow bricks of Yankton Rapids Memorial Hospital rose three stories behind an elm-shaded parking lot.

Angel stared at the glass-doored emergency-room entrance from the front seat of her rented car. Her face was expressionless, but her thoughts were churning over the stark unchangeable facts.

Serita had died before she reached that emergency entrance.

The young resident who had been on duty had known Jesse. There hadn't been any real problem in keeping the hospital records confidential. Jesse had been the one to talk to the press. He'd been terse, factual, grim, but his involvement with Serita, the newspapers had implied, had made the interview difficult. None of the reporters had probed too far.

Angel crossed her arms over the plastic steering wheel and leaned her forehead on her wrists.

Last night Jesse had made tender, passionate love to her. She had let him. She had let him make her forget the strange, unwanted knowledge of Serita's world and the chilling fact that Jesse seemed obsessed with it.

She'd wanted him to make her forget. She'd wanted him to love her. She'd needed his touch the way she needed music.

Now he was at the opposite end of Yankton Rapids's main street, at the ball field where they were setting up equipment for Serita's concert. She was alone with Serita's death, fighting an irrational fear that gnawed at her self-confidence and made the thought of performing at that concert terrifying.

They'd needed to do some work on the bandstand, Jesse had said. They expected an unprecedented crowd.

Angel hadn't wanted to be there. Five days from now, she would have no choice. She would have to walk out in front of that audience, Serita's audience, and sing. In tribute to her cousin. For an audience of boisterous and unruly fans who had idolized Serita. For people who were ready to start a brawl over a song on the jukebox.

A sense of panic nagged at her.

With an effort she ignored it, got out of the car and turned her back on the hospital.

Two months ago, she and everyone she knew believed Serita had died of a heart attack.

She had been the one who couldn't leave it at that. She was the one who'd needed to find out. She was the one who had auditioned to take Serita's place in Jesse's tour. She was the one who had demanded the truth.

Her hands closed into fists inside the pockets of her jeans.

And now she didn't know what she was going to do about it.

She pushed her hair back from her forehead and made herself take a deep, strengthening breath.

Across the street was the red brick structure of St. Mary's. The church basement was occasionally used, she knew, as a coffeehouse for folk music.

It was something that was safe and familiar, and it suggested something she could do to prop up her shaky confidence. She left her car and walked toward the red brick church. The flagstone walkway led her around to the side entrance. She followed it and found her way to the pastor's office.

Father Albert, a graying, soft-voiced man, was delighted with her offer to perform at a coffeehouse on Friday evening. Two phone calls later, the arrangements were in place.

Angel smiled at him, brushed off his thanks, and stood up to go, but when she reached the door she turned back. Her eyes studied the kindly, unassuming face for a moment, then she asked, on impulse, "Did you—know my cousin, Father?"

The priest's eyebrows rose in surprise, then he shook his head. "I knew who she was, of course. Everyone in these parts knew who she was. But she never came here."

Angel gave him a brief, self-conscious smile.

"Was she Catholic?" the priest asked, his eyes studying her.

"Yes. But—" Angel smiled again, then shrugged.

"I'll pray for her," the priest said quietly.

"Thank you."

She let herself out of the office and retraced her steps along the flagstones to the front of the church. She stood for a moment looking at the building.

She knew what kind of audience she'd find at the coffeehouse. Ordinary men and women—nice people. Like the people who would come to the benefit concert, she repeated doggedly to herself. Just people. She could reach them. She could sing for them.

She pushed her hands into the pockets of her jeans, let her eyes follow the lines of the church up to the spire of the bell tower, then back down again, to the scraggly lawn at her feet.

Her gaze moved up the street, past a few white clapboard houses toward the business district, the police station, the bars.

Just people.

At eight o'clock that evening, Angel stood at the edge of the stands behind third base, watching the distant figures on the stage of the grandstand. Jesse was directing the light crew. He snapped out orders with brusque authority, demanding perfection, brooking no compromise.

Even at a distance she could see that his face was drawn, the purple bruise at his temple dark and discolored.

"Jesse know you're here, honey?"

The voice was Nancy's. Angel turned, gave her an uneasy smile, and shook her head.

"He's been looking for you all day. He even left the setup, this afternoon." She grinned wryly. "He *never* leaves setups. He was gone two hours and he came back in a rotten mood, so I take it he didn't find you."

"I—was out. I haven't seen him since this morning."

The older woman gave her a measuring glance, her eyebrows raised.

Angel deflected the unasked question. "Has everyone else been here all day?"

Nancy nodded.

Angel's gaze moved back to the stage, then swept around the ball field, taking in the unfamiliar equipment crew, the recognized faces of Jesse's roadies, the small crowd of observers. On one side of the stands, a group of young men with the high cheekbones and black hair of their Indian ancestry sat drinking beer, tossing the empty cans down to the field. Across from them was a group from the town, rivaling them in boisterous high spirits, shouting occasional taunting insults at the Indians, which were returned with laughter that had a hostile edge.

Both groups were ignored by the crew.

Angel massaged her forehead with her fingertips, then, slowly, brushed her hair back from the sides of her cheeks. She glanced at Nancy. "I thought after last night, with Jesse being arrested, the concert might be canceled."

"Jack sweet-talked the promoters. They're still willing." The older woman's astute gaze rested on Angel for a moment before she said, with a little more than casual reassurance, "It's just a concert, honey, like every other one you've done."

Angel swallowed a sudden lump of anxiety in her throat. On the distant stage, Jesse jammed his hat on his head and called out another order to the light crew members.

"It's not just another concert to Jesse," Angel said, her voice tight.

Nancy's chest expanded with a deep breath. She put her hand on Angel's arm. "He went through hell when Rita died, honey. Maybe he needs to settle this his own way. Bear with him, okay?"

Angel's glance dropped. She wrapped her arms around her rib cage, hugging in the unresolved conflict, then looked away, toward the beer-drinking group on the bleachers.

"Maybe I need to settle it my own way, too, Nance." She turned back toward her parked car.

"Angel?"

"What?"

"You gonna leave without talking to him?"

Angel's mouth wrinkled in irresolution. "I don't know that talking will do any good. And anyway—" She didn't finish the sentence. She gave a small, hopeless shrug and walked toward her car.

The Red Hawk Café was an ancient, one-story structure with wooden clapboarding worn to the patina of old fence rails. The parking lot was half-full of cars and pickup trucks ranging from shiny new to derelict. It was a warm night. The door to the bar stood open, and the music of the jukebox floated out to the parking lot, along with a cloud of hazy smoke.

Music and smoke. Walking toward it, Angel had a flash of memory. Serita in the hay barn with one of the boys her parents disapproved of, playing her guitar and smoking forbidden cigarettes; herself and her nine-year-old best friend, Tammy, had hidden in the loft, looking on. They'd made a practice of spying on Serita, though they'd never given away her transgressions.

They hadn't needed to. Serita had always managed to get caught anyway.

The jukebox was turned up full volume. Angel walked past it and glanced around at the dim, noisy room. Her car keys were still clutched in her hand. She dropped them into her pocketbook and zipped the closure.

There were a couple of young women at one end of the long bar. She headed in their direction and took a stool near them.

The bartender, a big man with a no-nonsense air, ambled over in her direction and stopped in front of her, giving her a curious once-over. "What'll you have?" he asked.

"Beer."

"Draft?"

She nodded. "Yes, fine."

He brought it for her and she paid him, then took a nervous sip from the glass and set it down on the bar in front of her. The young women she'd sat near had stopped their conversation to glance toward her, but when she skimmed a look in their direction, they resumed their talk, ignoring her.

The song changed on the jukebox. The familiar opening gave her an uneasy shock. It was one of Jesse's. Angel glanced along the length of the bar, trying to imagine a brawl here, the police coming in, Jesse in the middle of it.

A boyish-looking beer drinker with curly brown hair and mischievous blue eyes was looking back at her. He got up, walked toward her and slid onto the stool next to her.

"Buy you a drink?" he said.

Angel gave him a nervous smile. "Actually, I was— looking for someone."

"Yeah?" He grinned at her. "Anyone in particular, or will I do?"

"Someone in particular. His name is Luke Standing Horse."

The blue eyes flickered toward the other side of the bar, then back to her, the look speculative.

"Is he here?" Angel asked.

"Hell, yes. He's always here." He tipped his chin toward one of the far tables and raised his voice. "Hey, Luke! You got a date!"

Angel followed the direction of his glance with a flush of embarrassment.

The two young women had stopped their conversation again. They were half-openly staring.

Luke Standing Horse ambled slowly toward her across the barroom, a beer bottle in one hand clutched by the neck. He was as tall as Jesse, thin, with jet-black hair, high, angular cheekbones, piercing black eyes. Beneath the insolent slouch, he had the spare, rangy grace of a Sioux warrior.

Angel's stomach tightened with an emotion she couldn't define. He and Serita, together, must have been a striking couple. For a moment, she was unable to speak.

The eyes of the man who had called Luke over moved from Angel's flushed, wide-eyed face to Luke's cynical, harsh appraisal. "You two know each other?" he asked with false congeniality.

Angel found her voice, held out her hand to the Indian, and said, too quickly, "I'm Angela Trent."

He glanced at her outstretched hand while he stood still as a statue. Then his head tipped back slightly and he laughed contemptuously. "Jesse's angel," he said.

Her hand hung in front of her, unshaken. She pulled it back and toyed with her glass of beer. "I'm Serita's cousin," she got out.

"I know who you are." Luke Standing Horse stared at her for a few seconds, then turned his stony gaze toward the curly-haired man who was still watching.

The man gave him a conciliatory smile, raised one palm, and moved away.

Luke took the newly vacant stool. He drank from the bottle in his hand, his eyes fixed on Angel, then reached into his shirt pocket for cigarettes and matches. He put a cigarette to his mouth and lit it. His eyes moved down over the length of Angel's body, then back up to her face. He was silent.

Jesse's rough, intimate voice from the jukebox filled the space between them.

She twisted the beer glass around in her hands. Luke Standing Horse was as hard and unapproachable as a hostile crowd. And she didn't have any clue as to how she might make a connection. All she could do was what she had come here for. She didn't have any of Jesse's familiarity with rough crowds.

She made herself meet Luke's hard black eyes. "I thought you might tell me something about her."

"Like what?" His lip curled. "How she died?"

"I know how she died."

The anger that flashed through Luke's piercing black eyes was gone so fast she almost thought she'd imagined it. He inhaled on the cigarette and blew out a stream of smoke.

"Does everyone else here know it?" she asked him.

He shrugged. "It wouldn't come as any great shock to anybody."

Angel let out a breath.

"It didn't come as any great loss, either," he said callously.

Her fingers tightened around the cold glass, clutching it. She snapped her head around toward Luke. "It was a loss to Jesse."

The Indian gave another cynical smile. "Maybe that was because he lost her earlier. In a poker game."

Something must have shown in her face. Luke's eyebrows rose. "That shock you, Angel?" He leaned an elbow on the bar. "I guess you haven't been around Jesse that long."

She looked away from him quickly, keeping her gaze fixed on the beer glass in front of her.

"Did you know he was here last night?" Luke asked.

She glanced at him and looked away again.

"He was buying drinks for one of the girls."

She felt heat creep up on her neck, all the more unwanted because she knew it was the kind of reaction Luke was pushing for. The song had changed on the jukebox. Serita's voice flowed out from the speaker.

The voice was so familiar, the sense of Serita's presence so strong, that Rita could have been in the room. Dizziness washed over her. The smoke was making her eyes burn. Angel glanced at Luke again. "I shouldn't have come here." She made a move to get up.

"So why did you?" There was a silence. Luke Standing Horse leaned a little closer to her, blocking her exit. "You trying to follow in Serita's footsteps?"

Angel gazed back at him.

The bartender, who'd been perched on a stool at one end of the bar, got up and walked by them. He stood leaning on the end of the bar near the door, watching them casually, arms crossed.

Luke Standing Horse ignored him, his gaze fixed on Angel. "You got Rita's place in the band," he drawled. "You got her place with Jesse." His mouth curled. "You want to take it one step further? We could go back to my house. I'd be happy to oblige.''

She stood up quickly, her lips pressed in a thin line, and started around behind him toward the door.

Luke's iron-strong fingers closed around her arm, stopping her. "Okay," he said, his face inches from hers. "I'll wait my turn. Maybe Jesse'll feel like playin' more poker.''

Angel yanked at her arm. Luke held her for a moment longer, then, with insolent leisure, let her go.

In front of the door, the bartender swung around toward the entrance and put his burly hand on the chest of Jesse Adam Wilson, who was framed in the doorway. "No way, pal," he said. "You're not coming in here tonight."

Jesse flung his arm off without even a glance. His attention was on Angel and Luke. He took a step toward them.

The bartender stepped in front of him again, arm raised to block his progress.

She saw Jesse's muscles tense, his still-bandaged fingers close into a fist.

Luke had spun around on the bar stool. The two girls at the bar were watching avidly.

There was a sick feeling in the pit of Angel's stomach. "No!" She flung the word out before she could stop herself.

Without thinking, she dashed toward Jesse, grabbed at his arm, and tried to pull him away from the potential fight.

His hands closed around her shoulders, hard enough to hurt. "What the hell are you doing here?" he demanded.

He had no right to ask, but it cut to the heart of her own fears. She should never have come here. She didn't belong.

Luke Standing Horse had gotten up and was moving toward them, his face set in a sneer that she knew would be the spark to fire Jesse's anger.

Her stomach was twisted with tension that had crossed the line to becoming unbearable. She wrenched away from

Jesse, turned on her heel and ran from the confrontation, the potential violence, and her own raw emotions.

"Angel, dammit." Jesse went after her. He caught up with her as she reached the car and put a hand on her arm. She flinched away from him.

He let go of her, flinging his hand up with a frustrated, angry gesture. "I've been driving around town for an hour, looking for your car. I didn't know where the hell you were. I didn't know where you were all day."

"I can't do it, Jesse." She fumbled in her handbag, frantic, searching for car keys.

"Angel—"

"I'm not doing it!" Her fingers closed around the keys, and she snatched them out of the handbag. "I'm not doing the concert."

"Angel, dammit—"

She grabbed at the door handle. Jesse put his hand on the car door to shut it. "Angel, what the hell happened in there?"

"There was almost another f-fight." Her voice was shaking.

"No, there wasn't."

"Y-you were—"

"I was looking for you, for God's sake!"

She snatched at the door handle again and pulled it against Jesse's arm. He cursed and let go of the door. "I'll drive," he said as she swung it open.

"No." She shook her head vehemently.

"Angel, you can't even—"

"I'm f-fine." But as she fumbled with the keys in the ignition, they dropped from her shaking fingers.

Jesse got in. His hip pushed her across the seat. She drew in a strangled breath and moved as far from him as possible, staring out the opposite window while he started the car, backed it around and drove out of the parking lot. He turned in the direction of the motel.

"I can't do it, Jesse," she said, speaking toward the window.

She felt him glance at her, heard the quick exhalation of his breath. "What did he say to you?"

She shook her head. "Nothing."

"It wasn't nothing!" he exploded. "Dammit, Angel, he was probably drunk."

"It wasn't just him!" She spun around toward Jesse, clutching her handbag as if it were a shield. "It's this whole town. It's the guys at the ball field throwing their beer cans, and the police, and the jukebox, and the—the church." Her voice broke. "I'm a f-folksinger, Jesse. I can't do this! They don't want to hear me. They don't want a folksinger. I can't—"

He pulled over to the curb of the road at the side of Main Street, jerked the car to a stop and jammed it into parking gear.

"Okay, talk."

She clamped her mouth shut.

Jesse spun around toward her, one hand on the steering wheel. "You think not talkin' about it is going to make it any easier?"

"No."

He reached for her. His hands on her shoulders turned her toward him. "Angel—"

"You don't understand any of this! The only thing that matters to you is the d-damn c-concert!"

"I understand stage fright when I see it."

"Stage fright!" Her voice thinned in outrage. "It's not stage fright! I booked another concert today, at the church. I didn't feel any stage fright about that!"

"Well, you do about this! Have you thought about how you'll feel if you give in to it this time? What do you think it's going to do for your career if you don't show?"

"I don't care!"

"Yes, you do. What do you think it's going to do to you if you get scared out of a performance?"

She tried to pull away, and his hands tightened on her shoulders. "You gonna spend the rest of your life singin' in church basements, Angel?"

"Maybe that's where I belong. Maybe that's what I was meant to do. I don't know anything about the kind of music this town wants to hear. I'm not Serita!" She stared at his grim, angry face, until his image wavered through brimming tears. "Dammit—" The word came out on a sob. "L-leave me alone!"

"To do what?" His hands tightened around her shoulders, and he shook her once, roughly. "Go back to your room and think about how you can't cut it in Serita's town?"

"What do you care what I think about?"

His fingers tightened more, gripping her shoulders. "It's my business to care. I'm putting on a concert Saturday night and you're booked to open for it."

"Oh, I know what your business is! You don't let anything get in the way of one more concert, do you?"

"It's not just one more concert. It's Serita's benefit concert, Angel." The rough voice was harsh and unforgiving. "It's what she did with her life. It's what she stood for."

"What she did with her life was end it with a cocaine overdose!" she flung at him, defiant and defensive.

"She did a lot more than that. She may have made some big mistakes, but they weren't the sum total of what she did with her life."

Angel stared at him through a haze of tears, her spine rigid, her mouth trembling. "Well, I don't care what else she did with it! Her life was a lie!"

He let go of her so abruptly she slumped back against the window like a dropped curtain. "Who are you to pass judgment on her?" Jesse rasped. "Who are you to talk about lies? What do you call backing out of a contract?"

She stared at him, biting her lip, silent, then jerked her head around toward the window.

With sudden violence, Jesse yanked the keys out of the ignition, shouldered open the car door, and got out. He flung the keys across the seat toward her, then bent down to lean into the car. "You can go back to church basements when this tour is done, Angel, but not before Serita's benefit."

He slammed the door hard enough to make her flinch, turned on his heel and stalked off along the sidewalk in the direction of the Red Hawk.

His footsteps echoed away into silence.

Alone in the darkened car, Angel stared straight ahead of her at downtown Yankton Rapids until the seedy main street wavered and blurred into a meaningless wash of garish color. Jesse's accusations were bitter in her mind, juxtaposed with her own bitter, unresolved feelings about her cousin and her own chaotic, churning panic.

In front of her, the neon sign of a package store blinked off and on, as if in mocking representation of her own inability to come to terms with her unfaced and undefeated fears.

Ten

The basement parish hall of Saint Mary's barely held a hundred folding chairs, crowded together on the tiled floor. All of them were taken. Latecomers were standing at the back of the room and along the sides. There were quiet murmurings while Angel tuned up, strummed a chord, said good evening and adjusted the microphones.

The mikes were borrowed from Jesse; Nancy had okayed the loan. Angel hadn't spoken to Jesse since he'd left after their argument.

But she'd needed his mikes. Her own were in storage in Nebraska, unused since her last solo tour. When this would have been a big audience.

She glanced around at the faces, noting the comfortable shabbiness of the setting, needing the reassurance of its familiarity. She had sung in hundreds of halls like this one, with painted steel columns supporting the ceiling, Sunday school bulletin boards pushed to one wall, coffee bubbling in church percolators. And audiences who wanted to hear folk music.

She played the opening riff of a well-known ballad, leaned toward the mike and started the song.

The small crowd was enthusiastic, polite, easy to please. She performed her standard coffeehouse repertoire, interspersing traditional music with her own compositions. The applause for each was warm, attentive, hearteningly encouraging.

There was little movement in the audience, even among the standing listeners at the back. When, halfway through an instrumental ballad, the crowd shifted to admit one more she glanced idly toward that corner of the room.

Luke Standing Horse walked through the door, let it shut behind him, and strolled up the side aisle. In front of the line of standees he leaned one shoulder against the side wall, his arms crossed in front of him. His piercing black gaze was fixed on Angel. His expression was one of arrogant appraisal.

Still playing, she stared back. Heads in the audience were beginning to turn to see what she was looking at. She caught herself, gave him a brief nod, and called her attention back to the guitar piece.

But the comfortable familiarity of the performance was shattered. When she had finished the song, she had to force herself not to look at him to see if he was applauding. When the applause died out, she had a sudden, panic-stricken realization that she didn't know what to do next.

I know stage fright when I see it, Jesse had said.

Her throat was dry and her heart was pounding in her chest, in a way that she couldn't help but recognize as stage fright.

Unexpectedly shaken, she made herself glance around the room, made her fingers form a chord and strum it, made herself look at the faces in the hall.

This was a folk audience. This was a church basement, not a concert auditorium. It was her sphere, a theater of her choosing. Deliberately, she turned her head enough to see Luke Standing Horse at the side of the room. He was staring back at her, his arms still folded across his chest, his eyes full of challenge.

She swallowed, tipped her chin up and met his gaze.

She had come here to sing. This was what she did, what she knew how to do, what she cared about. She put her innermost thoughts, her deepest feelings—her soul—into music. She was a singer and this audience had come here to listen to her. If Luke had come to listen then she owed him something to listen to.

Into the lengthening silence she said, "I want to do a song I don't usually sing for anyone. I wrote it for my cousin, Serita Black."

There was a surprised, attentive pause while she glanced around the room once again then and started the first, softly strummed notes.

The words came back to her, unfalteringly, though she hadn't sung them for more than a year. The melody caught her up as it spun itself effortlessly out through her fingers, pliant with feeling. She let her eyes slide shut, let her head tip back slightly, let herself feel the music.

She taught me how to play the songs of freedom
On a summer day beneath a wide blue sky.
I was greener than the valley by the river,
But I wanted her to teach me how to fly.

The road beyond that distant blue horizon
Gave me longings that I couldn't seem to lose,
But everything I ever knew of freedom
Was the cloud of dust that lifted from her shoes.

Her voice flowed over the words like water over a sand-strewed riverbed, summoning emotions she hadn't felt in a long time. The words drew a picture as vivid as war paint.... Serita, exotic in Angela's ten-year-old eyes, had had her guitar across her knees. Her gaze had been set fiercely and impatiently on the gravel road that led off behind the barn, toward town.

"You're not really gonna go, are you, S'rita?" Angel had asked.

Serita had laughed, with careless rebellion and excited, unfettered eagerness. "Sure I am," she'd said.

And surely she had. She had gone, now, for good....

As the song ended and she played out the last notes on the guitar, emotion shimmered in Angel's chest. It filled up a hollow, aching sense of loss she hadn't known she still felt.

A wave of fervent applause brought her back to the present. She opened her eyes and scanned the room with a smile of thanks.

Luke Standing Horse was no longer in the audience.

But at the back of the hall, behind the crowd, Jesse Adam Wilson stood in the doorway, applauding, watching her, his gaze direct, unapologetic and intense.

Her heart started to pound again. She wrenched her eyes away from him. I know stage fright when I see it, he had said. But this wasn't stage fright. It was something at once more fundamental and more complex. Something bound up with her deepest, most personal conflicts. There was no simple word to make it comprehensible, no technique to use for control. She only knew that somewhere along the path she had chosen she had put her heart into Jesse Adam Wilson's keeping, and she was scared.

When she put her hands back on her guitar they were shaking.

She didn't look toward him again through the rest of the concert, an encore, and while the small crowd of autograph seekers surrounded her after it was over. She signed programs, smiled, made polite comments to the people who spoke to her, but part of her mind, through it all, was riveted on the spot in the doorway where he'd been leaning against the jamb with careless grace, his shoulders propped against the door frame, his gaze following her movements.

She looked up, finally, to face him.

He was gone.

The morning of the scheduled concert, Saturday, dawned hazy, warm, and indifferent to Angel's state of mind as she stood looking out the motel window. Sleep had been impossible. She'd finally given up, thrown off the disheveled sheets and gotten out of bed. She stood now in her nightgown, drinking tea, trying to make a decision about the performance.

The brightening sky held no answers. She turned away from the window and went into the bathroom.

She stood under the shower long moments, her face tipped into the pelting stream of water as if it could wash away her fear and her confusion.

Finally she shut off the faucets, reached for a towel and wiped her face. She dried herself and pulled her nightgown back over her head. In the steamed mirror, her face looked pale, her eyes enormous, wary, shadowed with indecision.

Hair still wet and tangled, she left the bathroom to retrieve her cup of tea.

Someone was knocking on the outside door.

Frowning, she went to open it. Outside, Luke Standing Horse was waiting, his face unreadable in the early-morning light, his hands hanging still at his sides.

She made a small sound of surprise in the back of her throat.

Luke gazed at her impassively, his eyes moving from her wet hair to her cotton nightgown and bare feet. He nodded once. "You're up early." It was a flat statement.

"So are you," she said when he didn't continue.

"No." He gave her a quick, humorless smile. "I'm up late." His expression sobered again. "I spent the night...thinking. Of Serita. What I said about her in the Red Hawk." The dark eyes met hers, unblinking, steady. His voice was even. "What I said to you. I apologize for that. It was said out of anger that wasn't meant for you."

Angel shook her head and gave a small shrug of denial, her eyes wide, her hand still on the door. "That's not necessary."

"Yes." His mouth thinned. "It is."

Angel gazed at him, silent, caught in the strange, early-morning ambience of the moment. He seemed like a different man from the one she'd met in the bar. The impression of his Indian heritage was vivid and undeniable.

"The song you sang about her—got to me," he said. On the last words, he looked down and gave a huff of breath, at odds with the almost formal composure he'd shown so far. "When I said her death was no great loss—I was lying. It meant something to me. Her life meant something to me. I wanted you to know that. She took the same kind of background we all had and made good with it—turned it into a thing she could glorify. That meant something. To all of us."

Angel stared back at him, sensing that her silence was a more fitting answer than anything she could have said.

"I have a gift for you." He held out his hand. Dangling from his fingers was an amulet made of eagle feathers and beads hung on a leather thong.

She glanced at it, then looked back at Luke's face, her eyes wide. She gave him a swift, questioning smile.

"Eagle feathers," he said. "I was going to sell them, and the ones they came with. I decided last night not to."

Angel reached up and took the amulet, holding it carefully, staring at the fragile, intricate beadwork, the long, white-tipped feathers. She glanced at Luke again, still speechless.

"Four feathers," he said. "Four is a sacred number to the Sioux." He glanced down at her again. "It's a gift that should be given at dawn."

Over Luke Standing Horse's shoulder, the first yellow rays of the sun were streaming over the low, grass-clad hills east of town. Angel's gaze moved to his impassive, unsmiling face. "Thank you," she said.

Nancy was at the soundboard and the crew was setting up amps and monitors when Angel arrived at the outdoor stage of the ball park. The afternoon sun slanted over the bleachers of the infield and glinted on the mike stands still grouped at the center of the stage. Jesse was standing behind them, facing away from her, talking to Jack.

At the edge of the stage, Angel set her guitar case down on the wooden platform, took out her guitar and looped the strap over her shoulders. She walked across the stage toward Jack and Jesse. In her left hand, half-hidden in the folds of her fawn-colored suede dress, she carried Luke's eagle feathers. Jesse turned as she approached.

She stopped in front of him and tipped her chin up to meet his eyes. "I want to open tonight with you and the band," she said evenly.

Jack's eyebrows rose in question.

Jesse's face didn't change. He gazed back at her for a few seconds, then reached for one of the mikes, pulled it toward him, and spoke into it.

"We need a sound check, Nance, on Angel and me with the band."

At the board, Nancy's head snapped up. She lifted one hand off the sound panel and pushed her hair back off her face. "To open?" she called down to them.

"Yeah." Jesse glanced over his shoulder at Jack. "Tell everybody we need 'em here, okay?"

Jack nodded, gave Angel a surprised, respectful glance, and turned away toward the wings.

Jesse looked back to her, taking in her resolute gaze, the set of her mouth, the decided line of her shoulders. His eyes fell on the eagle feather amulet that hung from her fingers, and his eyebrows rose in question.

"It was a gift," she said. She threaded the leather thongs behind the strings on the neck of her guitar and reached with both hands to tie them. "From Luke Standing Horse."

Jesse didn't answer, but his silence had a quality of understanding that didn't need to be spoken.

Hank and Carlos were coming across the stage toward the mikes, Hank with his bass slung over his shoulder.

"What do you want to open with?" Jesse asked Angel.

"One of Serita's songs." She drew in a breath. " 'Hope and Dreams.' "

She watched the play of expression across Jesse's face: surprise, evaluation and quick, fundamental respect.

He turned back to the microphone. "We're doing 'Hope and Dreams,' Nance. Keep the instruments down. We'll want to hear Angel's voice." He glanced around at the members of his band, assembling themselves, moving mikes, tuning strings, then looked back at her. "How do you want to arrange it, Angel?"

"Do it the way you used to do it with Rita."

His gaze rested on her face a moment longer, then he slowly smiled. "Okay," he said over his shoulder. "Take it from the top, boys."

Four hours later Angel walked out on stage in front of Jesse, to a sound made by the hands and voices of eleven thousand people. The applause rose in a wave around her, like the sound of one enormous voice. The stands were full. She couldn't make eye contact with any single listener; there were no seats close enough to the stage. But she could feel the emotions from this crowd—volatile, close to the surface, already at the fever-pitch of intensity that Jesse's audiences sometimes reached when he chose to loose his control.

She moved her hand on the neck of her guitar so that her fingers brushed the beadwork of her eagle feathers, and she glanced around the huge audience, listening to the applause die down, trying to judge the moment she should start. She wasn't sure...she didn't know how to judge a crowd like this.

Behind her, the notes of Jesse's guitar started the intro, solid and certain, leading in the rest of the band like the workings of well-oiled machinery. Before her fears had claimed any more of her ability, she was singing.

"All I am is hope and dreams..."

Serita's song. Serita's words. Angel's voice was as unlike her cousin's as shadow is to sun, but her pure, rich soprano held the words as if they had been written for her, and gave them a poignancy of meaning that had never been part of Serita's dark, world-weary rendition of the song.

Hope and dreams and hangin' on
Waiting for the light of dawn,
Knowin' what you had is gone
And never knowing why.

You only do the best you can,
You never get to see the plan.
The thing I've come to understand
Is how to say goodbye.

It seemed as if she could feel Serita's presence on the stage, as if her singing could evoke Serita's spirit and give voice to a meaning in her song that had been eclipsed by the troubled darkness of her cousin's life.

For Angel, the performance was a release of ambivalence and resentment, a freedom of her own spirit, a gift to her cousin. While she sang she was unaware of the stage, the sound equipment, the crowd listening. When the last notes hung in the air, ethereal and vanishing, she stood for a few seconds in weighted silence, glancing around at the huge, unnaturally hushed audience, not knowing how to read the reaction.

There was a sudden, thunderous burst of applause and a monolithic ovation of voices. She stood for a stunned moment of incomprehension before she realized the import of the sound.

She and Jesse had planned to alternate songs, but when she turned away from the mike, he was standing with his guitar slung loosely over his shoulder, grinning at her. He stepped closer and leaned to speak into her ear over the sound of the continuing applause.

"Better do another one, Angel."

She glanced at him, startled, looked out at the audience, then back at Jesse, while a slow smile spread across her face. She nodded. "Okay. Can you follow me?"

He grinned again. "I can follow you anywhere, Angel."

They played for three and a half hours. Long after the last encore, the drawn-out ovation, the bustle of clearing the stands and packing up equipment, Angel stayed where she was. She watched the denouement of Serita's concert, accepted the congratulations of the band, Jack, Nancy, the crew and steadfastly refused their offers of celebration.

It was past midnight when the darkened stage was empty, the instruments removed, the audience dispersed. She sat by herself on a stage stool, her guitar beside her.

She was waiting for Jesse, she realized. It didn't surprise her when he appeared from the wings and walked toward her across the stage.

His cut lip had healed. The bruise at his temple was all but invisible. There was no overt sign of the confrontation that had preceded this concert, but beneath the easy grace of movement she could detect the tension in the lithe body.

He stopped when he was ten feet away from her, stood silent for a moment, then smiled a ghost of his outlaw's grin. "You were damn good," he said. "You were better than Serita ever was. You're better than she ever would have been."

"Thanks," she said finally. She looked out toward the now empty and darkened stands. "It felt like . . . saying goodbye to her tonight."

"I know."

"I don't think it matters much anymore whether I'm as good as Serita. Whether I can measure up."

Jesse said nothing, but he watched her steadily, his gaze unwavering and direct. She felt something stir in the deepest part of her soul, like the uncurling of a living green shoot, spreading new leaves to the light of the sun. Her breathing quickened.

"What now, Angel?" he said softly.

She shrugged and gave him a brief, breathless smile. "I thought I'd spend a couple of days in Nebraska. We have some time off yet, and I thought—"

"I want to come with you."

"To Nebraska?"

"Nebraska, Texas, wherever you want to go."

Her eyes darkened in confusion, but her pulse started to race. "I don't—"

"I want to meet your family, Angel. They have a right to know who you're getting."

"Who I'm—" She let out a breath that could have been a laugh. "Who I'm getting for what?"

He didn't smile. "For life. For better or worse. Till death do us part."

Her nervous smile faded. Uncertainty, hope, hesitation and surging emotion were all fleetingly visible on her face. "It's not that simple, Jesse. We can't just—"

"It *is* that simple," he interrupted her. He stood straight-legged, hands on his hips, hat at a level angle over his direct gaze. "You want to live in Nebraska, we'll live in Nebraska. I'll buy a farm. You can show me how to run a tractor. I'll sing at the grange hall. I'll sell the bus."

She shook her head, watching him through wide, disbelieving eyes. "Jesse..."

He closed the distance between them with two long strides, leaned over her and tipped her chin up with one hand. His mouth met hers with gentle pressure, seductive, sensual and convincing. He kissed her until she yielded to the kiss, meeting his mouth with sensuality of her own, elicited by feelings deeper than the reasonable protests of common sense.

"Do you want me, Angel?" he murmured, his hand still cupping her chin, his voice rough and intimate.

"Yes," she said, the word barely a whisper.

The outlaw's grin crept up his face again. Her heart started to hammer in response to that grin, the force of will and talent behind it, her own longing for a life that would share that will and that talent.

"Yes," she repeated, more urgently.

"I like the sound of that," he told her, still grinning. His arm circled her shoulders and pulled her up from the stool. He tucked her against him, hip to hip, and started with her toward the edge of the stage. "You always say yes in my imagination, Angel."

His back felt warm and hard beneath his shirt as she slipped her arm around his waist. She spread her palm wide against his hip, while a heady sense of possession shot through her.

He walked her to the stairs at the edge of the stage. From the second step he leaned toward the stage platform, bending her with him, to pick up a folded blanket. She recognized it as one from the bus. Jesse must have brought it with him. He'd been pretty sure of himself, she thought. She started to smile. "Where are we going?"

"The picnic grove. Over there." The movement of his chin indicated a dark grove of cottonwood trees that bordered the creek, across an open field from the ballpark.

Her smile widened. He'd declared he'd follow her wherever she wanted to go, but he'd chosen their first destination without consulting her. "Oh, are we," she said.

He glanced at her quizzically.

"I thought we were going to Nebraska. To buy a farm and sing at the grange hall."

He stopped at the bottom of the stairs, turned her toward him and gazed down at her. His mouth was straight, and his eyes were shadowed under the hat, but she could sense the smile in his voice. "On our way to Nebraska would you come with me to the picnic grove, Angel Trent?"

His hands rested on her shoulders. She brought her own hands up to his hips, where her palms brushed slow, luxurious circles against the rough fabric. "I would love to come with you to the picnic grove, Jesse Wilson."

He smiled, slowly, then circled her shoulders with his arm again and started walking across the field.

Before they'd reached the middle of the field, the hem of Angel's suede dress was damp from the tall grass, but she was unconscious of it. All her awareness was attuned to the man beside her, his hip against her waist, his long, lean thigh brushing hers as they walked. The past few days, without him, had been long, but their walk across the field seemed longer still, rich as it was with her own anticipation. Jesse walked slowly, not hurrying, seemingly at ease, but she could hear his quickened breathing, and she knew his pulse was racing as fast as hers.

Her hand, on his hip, crept upward, and she slipped her fingers into the waistband at the side of his jeans.

His hand tightened on her shoulder, and he glanced down at her, grinning. "It's a long ways to that picnic grove," he said. The words were a slow drawl. His steps, still leisurely, didn't quicken.

"Is it?" she answered, equally casual. She worked her fingers lower inside the waist of his briefs, under the jeans.

"Yeah," Jesse said. His arm pulled her a little closer.

The side of her breast was pressed against Jesse's chest. Beneath the soft suede, she felt her nipple harden.

"And we're not going to get there," Jesse muttered. Abruptly, he dropped the blanket, pulled her into his embrace, and bent his head to hers. She met him, mouth to mouth, body to body, in a kiss that held no restraints, and as their tongues met and intertwined, hot, eager and impatient, the shadows of the woman that had kept them apart dissolved into a white, brilliant flare of passion.

The muscles in Jesse's strong back flexed as he pulled her against him, and the heel of his hand pressed into her spine, down along each vertebra to the small of her back. Against her stomach she could feel the hard ridge of his arousal.

Angel's emotions had been reined in by her own discipline, her desires leashed by her own fears, but now there was no need for holding back, and the knowledge was intoxicating. A font of sensuality seemed released inside her, as if she were overflowing with weighted, liquid desire. She moved against him, a slow circle of her hips, subtle, but guided by elemental feminine instinct.

Jesse's hands slid down to cup her curved buttocks in widespread palms. Supple suede whispered over resilient flesh as he kneaded and caressed, guiding her movements. A low growl of passion came from his throat. Her answering sound was lost in the kiss that still joined them.

When he lifted his head, his hands pulled her hard against him. "Ah...Angel...on stage, tonight, you were so good, I wanted to keep listening to you forever, but at the same time all I could think about was how much I wanted you...how much I wanted you like this...how much I wanted t'hear you say yes and keep sayin' it..."

In the luxurious private silence broken only by a breath of wind in the field grass and the distant rustle of cottonwoods, she smiled at him. "Yes," she said.

A slow smile curved his mouth. "There's a better way to say it. Without words."

"Yes, I think there is."

His hands moved again on her backside, bunching up the fabric of her dress, then letting the suede slide through his fingers in supple folds. "You have to take your clothes off to do it."

Her hands spanned his rib cage, then moved up over his chest to the open collar of his shirt. "And so do you, I think." She pulled open the first silver snap, then the second and the third. The rest came open with one tug, and when she slipped her hands inside Jesse's shirt to contour his broad chest, she could feel his heart thrumming in heated rhythm against his breastbone.

He circled her wrists with his strong fingers and brought her hands to his mouth to wet each palm with slow, sensual strokes of his lips and tongue.

Her dress was a slim sheath of leather held together by ties at the back. He turned her halfway around, still holding her wrists, like a square dancer executing a slow turn, then he released her hands, and his fingers slid under her hair to the nape of her neck to untie the first knot. When the dress was unfastened he pushed it forward over her shoulders. It slipped over her arms and caught around her hips, trapped between their bodies. With a single, deft tug, Jesse unhooked her bra and let it fall with the dress.

A breath of wind touched her skin with coolness, then her breasts were covered with Jesse's warm, wide palms. She pressed her own hands on top of his, pressing harder to fill the ache of need for his touch, though that touch only inflamed the longing.

"Jesse." She let her eyes slide shut and tipped her head back, leaning against his shoulder. "I've wanted this...I've wanted you to do this..."

"What do you want me to do?" he murmured gruffly. "Tell me."

In silence she turned toward him and reached up to circle the back of his head and pull it down to her waiting breast. His lips opened over the nipple, and she felt the warm, wet touch of his tongue. Her fingers tightened urgently, threading into his hair. He kissed, suckled, tugged with his mouth and the gentle pressure of his teeth. Angel made a sound of exquisite pleasure in the back of her throat and grasped his shoulders, leaning back to increase the pull of his mouth, then forward again when the pleasure grew too intense to bear.

Suddenly Jesse straightened and pulled her roughly against him. His hands moved ardently on her naked back, then brushed down to push the dress over her hips and thighs. His hands skimmed back up her body, dipping into the hollows of her hips, molding her rib cage, then circling under her breasts to lift their weight in each palm.

She reached for the snap of his jeans, pulled it open, tugged down the zipper, and Jesse's hands left her to yank

the jeans impatiently down from his hips. The snug denim
bunched at his knees. With a muffled curse, he dropped into
the grass on his backside and tugged off his boots, flinging
them, one at a time, over his shoulder.

Angel's smile curved again as she knelt in front of him
and reached for the blanket. "I guess we don't really need
to get to the picnic grove anyway," she said. She pulled the
blanket up in front of her, holding it tight under her chin as
she grinned at him teasingly. "Since you forgot the picnic
lunch."

His hands stopped tugging at the jeans for a moment as
his mouth quirked but didn't smile, then, with one final
yank, he pulled the jeans off and dropped them in front of
him. His eyes held hers as he reached a hand up to the brim
of his hat and sent it sailing after the boots into the tall
grass.

With one deliberate movement he snatched the blanket
away from her fingers, then, still watching her, spread it on
the grass beside her, his movements precise and elaborately
casual. Then, grinning, he pounced at her and knocked her
flat underneath him on the blanket. He worked one thigh
between her legs and settled himself against her, holding her
wrists pinned to the blanket beside her head. "Hungry, are
you?" He lowered his mouth to the side of her neck, nuz-
zling and nibbling, sending shivers of sensation radiating
through her.

She gave a breathless laugh, constrained by the pressure
of his broad chest against her flattened breasts. "I was just
thinking—"

His mouth traced a hot, moist trail from the curve of her
neck along her collarbone.

"How long it could take—to get to Nebraska—"

His tongue dipped into the hollow at the base of her
throat, then moved lower to the hollow between her breasts.
Her voice trailed off and she waited, breathless, for his

mouth to trace a curving path along the underside of one breast, then move upward toward the crest. His lips closed round the nipple, and her breath escaped in a low moan of passion.

Jesse moved over her, then released her wrists and twined his fingers into the hair at the nape of her neck. He plundered her mouth with his kiss, his tongue thrusting into the silken reaches with urgent, imperative need.

The stars far above Jesse's shoulder glittered in brilliant pinpoints of light, and the grass beneath them whispered and murmured as Jesse's body pressed down onto hers, fitting himself against her, starting the slow, sensual movements of his hips that found their answering cadence in her own rhythm of sensuality.

She wrapped her arms around his strong back and widened the cradle of her thighs to mold their hips more closely. "Ah, Jesse..." she murmured into his mouth. Then, as he joined their bodies together, "Yes...yes..."

Their rhythm was synchronized, perfect, instinctive. His music flowed through her veins and pulsed in her heart; her song surrounded and enveloped him, exquisitely beautiful, until the composition expanded in the ancient, beautiful rhythm of physical love, cadence by cadence, higher...higher...building to the inexorable, inevitable culmination in music of muscle and nerve, flesh and blood. Angel clutched at Jesse's shoulders as she felt the first quiver of release deep within her. Jesse's hands grasped her hips to raise her higher against the thrust of his strong body, and she felt herself dissolve in a quivering ecstasy of sound and light and sensation, her own cry of release echoed and given back in Jesse's low, rough, utterance of love, fulfillment and possession.

Their voices and the music echoed away into image and the imprint of memory. A gust of air rustled its way through the tall grass of the field to touch their damp skin, then continued on to murmur in the cottonwoods. The stars shimmered silently.

"Jesse..." Angel said, whispering it.

He lifted his head from where it had fallen on her shoulder. "Hmm?" He crooked an elbow to prop his head on his hand, but his weight was still on her, as welcome, for the moment, as the darkness and the quiet.

She smiled at him slowly. Her languid fingers caressed the back of his neck. "I'm not hungry anymore."

His teeth flashed in the darkness. "But you might be again soon." He ran a fingertip along her hairline and traced a lazy curlicue along the back of her ear and down her neck. "Do they have picnic groves in Nebraska, do you suppose?"

"Oh, I suppose so."

His lips replaced his fingertip in its sensuous path along her jaw. His breath fanned her cheek as he muttered against it. "I have a feeling it will be hungry country, Nebraska."

"Jesse..."

"Hmm." He kissed the corner of her mouth.

"I can't run a tractor."

He brushed her lower lip with his own, tracing the full, slightly swelled curve, then lifted his head so that his face hovered a fraction of an inch over hers. "Marry me anyway, Angel."

She felt the first trickle of desire returning, building again, like a half-conceived melody.

Jesse..."

He traced her upper lip, then kissed the opposite corner of her mouth.

"Don't sell the bus."

"Angel..." His mouth opened over hers, and the tip of

his tongue flicked over her lips before he drew back again.
"Marry me."

Without words, she told him yes.

*   *   *   *   *

FOUR UNIQUE SERIES
FOR EVERY WOMAN YOU ARE ..

Silhouette Romance

Love, at its most tender, provocative,
emotional . . . in stories that will make you laugh and
cry while bringing you the magic of falling in love.

6 titles per month

Silhouette Special Edition

Sophisticated, substantial and packed with
emotion, these powerful novels of life and love will
capture your imagination and steal your heart.

6 titles per month

Silhouette Desire

Open the door to romance and passion. Humorous,
emotional, compelling—yet always a believable
and sensuous story—Silhouette Desire never
fails to deliver on the promise of love.

6 titles per month

Silhouette Intimate Moments

Enter a world of excitement, of romance
heightened by suspense, adventure and the
passions every woman dreams of. Let us
sweep you away.

4 titles per month

SILG-1R

READERS' COMMENTS ON SILHOUETTE DESIRES

"Thank you for Silhouette Desires. They are the best thing that has happened to the bookshelves in a long time."
—V.W.*, Knoxville, TN

"Silhouette Desires—wonderful, fantastic—the best romance around."
—H.T.*, Margate, N.J.

"As a writer as well as a reader of romantic fiction, I found DESIREs most refreshingly realistic—and definitely as magical as the love captured on their pages."
—C.M.*, Silver Lake, N.Y.

"I just wanted to let you know how very much I enjoy your Silhouette Desire books. I read other romances, and I must say your books rate up at the top of the list."
—C.N.*, Anaheim, CA

"Desires are number one. I especially enjoy the endings because they just don't leave you with a kiss or embrace; they finish the story. Thank you for giving me such reading pleasure."
—M.S.*, Sandford, FL

*names available on request